Mortals of Kandahar III :

The Past

- Garima Yadav

The Past

Acknowledgments

Writing Mortals of Kandahar III: The Past has been a journey unlike any other—a dive into history, a relentless pursuit of untold stories, and an exploration of the people and events that shaped a forgotten world. This book would not have been possible without the unwavering support, guidance, and encouragement of many individuals who stood by me through every challenge.

First and foremost, my deepest gratitude goes to my family. To my husband, whose strength and unwavering belief in me have been my anchor; to my daughter, whose laughter and light remind me of the beauty in every story; and to my parents, whose love, wisdom, and encouragement have shaped the person I am today.

Their unwavering support has been the foundation upon which I stand. To my loved ones, who have supported me in ways both big and small—this book is as much yours as it is mine.

To my readers—you are the heart of Mortals of Kandahar. Your enthusiasm, your messages, and your relentless curiosity have fuelled my passion to keep writing. Thank you for stepping into this world with me, for embracing Aryanath and Kyra's journey, and for breathing life into these pages.

To the historians, scholars, and researchers whose works have guided me—your dedication to preserving the past has been invaluable. This book is a tribute not only to history itself but to those who ensure it is never forgotten.

To my friends and well-wishers, who have listened patiently as I rambled about ancient trade routes, political shifts, and temple archives—your patience, encouragement, and excitement have been a source of strength.

And finally, to Kandahar—the land of stories, of resilience, of an undying spirit. Through the centuries, its past has whispered to those willing to listen.

I hope, in some small way, this book has done justice to those whispers.

With gratitude,

Garima

<u>Synopsis</u>

In a time of shifting empires and vanishing legacies, Mortals of Kandahar III: The Past unearths the origins of two of history's most enigmatic figures—Aryanath and Kyra. Before they became the revered Scholars of Kandahar, before their names were etched into legend, they were seekers of truth navigating a world teetering on the brink of change.

Set against the turbulent backdrop of 9th-century Kandahar, this gripping historical epic follows Aryanath and Kyra as they unravel the mysteries buried within the city's ancient walls. As the influence of the Abbasid Caliphate wanes and new powers emerge, their journey leads them through treacherous landscapes—silk-laden trade routes, sacred temples, and hidden chambers where history itself is safeguarded. Alongside trusted allies and formidable foes, they confront betrayal, shifting alliances, and the ever-present threat of war.

But this is more than a story of survival. It is a tale of duty and sacrifice, of bonds forged in fire, and of an unbreakable connection that defies time. Through secret passages and sacred scrolls, Aryanath and Kyra unearth the very knowledge that will one day define them. Yet, in the shadows of history, fate demands a price—one that will shape the destiny of Kandahar forever.

As the final instalment before the events of Mortals of Kandahar, this novel brings the past full circle, weaving a narrative that connects the forgotten whispers of history to the legends yet to be told. Secrets will be revealed. Fates will be sealed. And the echoes of the past will finally find their voice.

Table of contents

Into THE PAST

Chapter 1: Veil of the Ancients

The wind rolled low across the plains of Kandahar, dry and heavy with dust, carrying the faint scent of sand and stone. Dawn crawled across the horizon in muted golds and silvers, struggling to break through the thick haze clinging to the land. The air was sharp with the bite of early winter, and the sky above the Koh-i-Suleiman mountains was a dull, washed-out blue, streaked with thin bands of cloud that moved sluggishly, as though reluctant to leave the peaks.

Aryanath tugged his woolen cloak tighter against his shoulders as he guided his horse along a narrow path, its hooves kicking up dry, brittle soil. The ancient road wound through the outer hills of Kandahar—land long abandoned, where only ruins and memories survived. Stone cairns dotted the ridges, worn smooth by centuries of wind, their meanings forgotten.

The silence here was different—not peaceful, but heavy.

Aryanath's dark eyes scanned the ravine ahead, where the earth split into a jagged wound, revealing the remnants of an ancient structure half-swallowed by sand. From this distance, the temple looked like the ribcage of some great beast, its pillars broken and leaning, the entrance partially collapsed beneath layers of stone and time.

He dismounted, boots crunching over loose gravel, and let his horse stay nearby. The path to the ruin was too steep, too treacherous for the animal to follow.

"Kyra," he called, his voice low but carrying in the dry air.

She emerged from behind a ridge, her presence calm yet commanding, and her form partially hidden beneath a long, hooded robe. Kyra always preferred the high ground—an old habit from their earlier days, before either of them had taken up the mantle of a scholar.

Kyra's lineage bore the weight of forgotten kingdoms. Born to a royal bloodline with mixed Greek origins, she carried the legacy of a family that once bridged cultures and empires. Her ancestors had ruled minor satrapies in the region-Hellenistic rulers who had stayed behind long after Alexander's armies had retreated. But dynasties crumbled, alliances broke, and Kyra had been left to navigate a world where her heritage was both a weapon and a burden.

Her sharp eyes flicked from the temple to Aryanath. "It's older than we thought," she said, brushing dust from her hands. Her dark hair, braided loosely, was streaked with dust, but her eyes were alert, always calculating, always searching. Beneath the heavy fabric of her cloak, she moved with the control of someone who had learned the weight of survival before the comfort of knowledge.

"Pre-dynastic?" Aryanath asked.

Kyra crouched, running her fingers through the dry soil, picking out shards of pottery and fragments of carved stone.

"Older. Before the Saffarids. Before the Caliphate's reach even touched Kandahar."

Aryanath's jaw tightened. They were on the trail of something significant—something buried so deep that even the Caliphate's endless hunger for knowledge and power hadn't uncovered it.

They descended into the ravine, boots sliding over loose rock, dust rising in clouds with every step. As they neared the temple's fractured archway, Aryanath noticed the strange carvings etched deep into the remaining stones—symbols twisted in spirals and interlocking lines, neither purely Buddhist nor Hindu. It was Kandahar's hybrid faith, the remnants of older beliefs before borders and empires had drawn clean lines between gods.

Kyra stopped at the base of the ruin, brushing her hand across a deep groove in the stone—an emblem half-worn by time. It was a circle, broken at its edges, with a blade running through its heart.

"The Gravekeepers," she whispered.

Aryanath's brow furrowed. "They still guard this place?"

"Or what lies beneath it."

The Gravekeepers were more myth than memory—an ancient sect, formed before the Silk Road turned Kandahar into a nexus of trade and conquest. Their sole purpose had been to guard sacred sites, especially those believed to hold relics or knowledge deemed too dangerous to fall into the hands of kings or warlords. But time had warped them. What had once been a brotherhood of preservation had rotted into fanaticism. Now, the Gravekeepers killed not to protect knowledge, but to keep it hidden forever.

A soft metallic scrape broke the air—like a blade dragged slowly across stone.

Kyra drew her dagger in a swift, fluid motion, its worn iron blade catching the pale morning light. Aryanath followed, his sword heavier but just as practiced in his grip.

From the shadows beneath the temple's ruined arch, figures emerged—three of them, cloaked in deep earth-colored robes, their faces masked by dark veils that left only their eyes exposed. Their armor was crude but thick—layered with hammered iron plates sewn into worn leather, built more for endurance than elegance.

One of them spoke, his voice muffled by the mask. "This ground is cursed by the old gods. Leave."

Aryanath didn't lower his blade. "We seek knowledge, not war."

"There is no knowledge here. Only death."

Kyra stepped forward, her tone calm but sharp. "If that were true, you wouldn't still be here, guarding it."

The Gravekeepers didn't answer.

Instead, the leader raised a curved scimitar in a slow, deliberate motion—a warning.

Aryanath's grip tightened around his hilt. He didn't want this fight. The Gravekeepers were bound by ancient laws, but those laws had twisted with time, and now their devotion made them dangerous.

The first strike came fast. One of the cloaked figures lunged, his blade arcing toward Aryanath's shoulder. Steel clashed with steel as Aryanath met the blow, forcing it wide. The sharp metallic ring echoed through the ravine.

Kyra moved like water, fluid and precise.

She ducked low, sweeping her dagger upward in a tight arc that sliced through one of the Gravekeeper's arm guards, the blade biting into flesh.

The leader swung at Aryanath again, faster this time, aiming for his exposed side. Aryanath pivoted, letting the blade glance off his shoulder guard before slamming his sword's hilt into the man's ribs. The Gravekeeper staggered but didn't fall.

"Kyra!" Aryanath called.

She was already moving. With a swift kick, she sent one of the attackers tumbling into the loose rock, dust billowing as he fell.

The last Gravekeeper hesitated—but only for a moment—before Aryanath's blade found its mark, cutting deep. The man gasped, falling hard against the temple's base.

Only the leader remained, chest heaving beneath his layered armor.

Aryanath stepped forward, sword raised. "We don't have to end this here."

But the man only lowered his mask, revealing sunken eyes, hollowed by time and belief. "It's already ended."

With that, he let himself fall backward into the ravine, his body swallowed by shadows below.

Silence returned, heavier than before.

Aryanath sheathed his sword, breath ragged. "They're hiding something deeper than relics."

Kyra glanced at the crumbling temple, its stones heavy with secrets. "And whatever it is... they were willing to die for it."

The mist swirled low once more, curling around the temple ruins like a veil being drawn tighter, as if the land itself resisted being uncovered.

Chapter 2: The Silent Keepers

The dust still hung in the air, thick and heavy, settling into the deep crevices of the temple ruins. The ravine was silent now—eerily so—except for the distant cry of a hawk circling high above the jagged cliffs. Aryanath adjusted the weight of his cloak, his breath still steadying after the fight with the Gravekeepers. The sharp, dry wind carried the faintest metallic tang of blood, lingering like a warning.

Kyra stood at the edge of the ravine, her amber eyes fixed on the shadows below where the last Gravekeeper had fallen. There was no sign of his body—only the gash in the stone where he had slipped into the depths.

"These Gravekeepers," Aryanath began, "they weren't just guarding the ruins. They were guarding something buried beneath."

Kyra nodded, brushing stray strands of hair from her face as the wind tugged at her cloak. "Their presence here isn't random. Kandahar's history is layered—Persian dynasties, Buddhist sanctuaries, Hindu shrines, and now the shadow of the Caliphate. This place has always been a crossroad."

She crouched at the crumbling stone arch, brushing away dirt to reveal a faint inscription—worn but still legible. The script was Brahmi, older than the current Persian-Arabic texts that dominated the region.

"'To those who remember the past, beware its weight,'" Kyra read aloud.

Aryanath frowned. "A warning?"

"Or a testament. This was built before the Saffarid dynasty took power—when Buddhist monasteries still thrived here. Before they were torn down or repurposed."

The Saffarids, under Ya'qub ibn al-Layth al-Saffar, had risen from humble beginnings—a coppersmith who forged a dynasty through sheer force and will. His expansion into regions like Kandahar in the late 9th century brought both prosperity and destruction. Temples were razed, libraries burned, and yet, in hidden places like this, relics survived—protected by those who saw knowledge as sacred.

Kyra traced the stonework, recognizing signs of Buddhist craftsmanship—carved lotuses and half-erased depictions of Bodhisattvas—mixed with newer symbols etched during later occupations. It was a palimpsest of faiths and empires.

They moved deeper into the ruins, the narrow passageway leading to what once might have been a prayer hall. Light filtered through a crack in the ceiling, illuminating weathered frescoes along the walls—scenes of merchants, pilgrims, and monks, painted during Kandahar's prime as a hub on the Silk Road.

But something else caught Aryanath's eye—a series of stone tablets, arranged along the back wall, their surfaces covered in text. Unlike the decorative carvings, these were records—edicts, trade agreements, and temple decrees.

"Look at this," Aryanath said, gesturing Kyra over.

She examined the closest tablet. "It's a ledger," she murmured, scanning the inscriptions. "Shipments of silk, lapis lazuli, and spices... but there's more—mentions of scholars traveling between Taxila and Kandahar, and a reference to a scroll repository."

Aryanath's brow furrowed. "A hidden archive?"

"Possibly. The Silk Road wasn't just about goods—it was about ideas. Philosophies, languages, technologies—they all passed through Kandahar. And when the Saffarids came, many of these scholars vanished."

"Or they went underground," Aryanath added.

They followed the ledgers to a narrow stone staircase leading beneath the main hall. The air grew colder here, dense with the smell of damp stone. Lantern light flickered across the rough walls as they descended, their footsteps hollow against ancient steps.

At the base of the stairwell, they found themselves in a cavernous chamber—half storage, half sanctuary. Shelves carved directly into the stone walls held scrolls and clay tablets, while the remnants of smashed statues littered the floor, their faces defaced.

"Iconoclast raids," Kyra whispered, brushing dust from a fragment of a broken

Buddha. "During the rise of the Saffarids, religious symbols were targets."

But something else caught her eye—an iron seal embedded in the wall, its surface engraved with the emblem of a forgotten dynasty.

"A Kushan mark," she breathed.

The Kushan Empire had once stretched from Central Asia into parts of India, and Kandahar had been a vital city in their network. Kyra's mixed Greek heritage gave her a deep understanding of the Hellenistic influences left behind by Alexander's campaigns, but here, in this hidden chamber, the Kushan presence was undeniable.

She pried the seal loose, revealing a hollow cavity behind it. Inside was a scroll—its edges frayed but the ink still dark.

Aryanath glanced over her shoulder. "What does it say?"

Kyra read silently before answering. "It's

a record of temple guardians—appointed not just to protect religious relics, but knowledge. Philosophical texts, medicinal scrolls, maps of ancient trade routes."

Aryanath's gaze hardened. "The Caliphate would have destroyed this."

"Or twisted it for their own use."

They weren't alone in their search. Across the region, emissaries of the Caliphate still scoured the remnants of Buddhist monasteries and Zoroastrian fire temples, hunting for anything that could strengthen their expanding empire.

A sudden, muffled sound echoed through the chamber—footsteps.

Aryanath motioned for silence, pulling Kyra behind a crumbling pillar as shadows passed across the stairwell. Three men emerged, dressed not as Gravekeepers, but as mercenaries—likely hired by local warlords or perhaps even the Caliphate itself.

"They're after the scrolls," Kyra mouthed.

Aryanath's hand tightened around his sword, but Kyra shook her head. "Not here. The noise would collapse this place."

Instead, they moved in the shadows, careful and deliberate, slipping behind broken shelves and statues until they reached another exit—a narrow tunnel that led upward, its steps slick with moisture from an underground spring.

As they emerged into the cold air above, Kyra turned back for one last glance at the ruins.

"This isn't just about relics," she said.

"It's about control. Whoever holds the past shapes the future."

Aryanath nodded grimly. "And we've just scratched the surface."

The sun was now high above the ravine, its light harsh against the jagged rocks, but there was a new weight in the air—something deeper than ancient stone. The knowledge buried beneath Kandahar was not lost. It was hidden. And now, it was stirring.

Chapter 3: The Shattered Oath

The sun's glare softened as twilight approached, casting long shadows across the weathered hills of Kandahar. The air, thick with dust, carried the faint scent of dry grass and smoke—remnants of fires long extinguished. Aryanath and Kyra moved through the winding gorge, where broken stones whispered of forgotten dynasties, their history buried beneath layers of conquest and silence.

The path led them deeper into the heart of the ancient ruins, where a once-magnificent vihara stood, its stone walls fractured by time and conflict. The faint etchings of Kharosthi inscriptions still lingered on the temple walls, weathered but defiant, a testament to Kandahar's role as a crossroad of cultures. Statues of Bodhisattvas, their faces eroded beyond recognition, lined the crumbling archways, watching as the last threads of the past unraveled.

Kyra, her cloak trailing the dusty ground, stopped before an altar blackened by fire. "The Guardian's mark," she murmured, pointing to the faint outline of an open hand etched into the stone.

Aryanath traced the symbol with his fingers. "The Temple Guardians swore to protect these archives. But someone shattered that oath."

Kyra's gaze hardened. "A betrayal strong enough to bury history."

The heavy silence was broken by the soft scrape of stone—footsteps echoing within the ruins. Aryanath gestured for silence, pulling Kyra into the shadows.

Two figures emerged from the shadows of a collapsed wall. Both were cloaked, their steps purposeful. One was tall and broad-shouldered, a curved sword slung low on his hip. The other moved with a deliberate calm, her dark braid tucked beneath a faded hood.

Aryanath recognized the sigil stitched onto the man's cloak—a hawk in flight. "That's Sifraan," he whispered to Kyra, his voice low. "He was once part of the Kandahar garrison before defecting."

Sifraan, known for his brutal tactics during the border conflicts, had been exiled for his refusal to follow orders that would have spared civilians. His reputation as a rogue strategist had since grown, his allegiances murky.

Kyra's eyes shifted to the woman. "And the other?"

"Samira," Aryanath replied. "A desert tracker. She's known for finding what others bury."

Samira had grown up in the fringes of the Sistan deserts, where survival meant understanding the land better than anyone else. She had once been a caravan guide, until the Saffarid expansion turned trade routes into battlegrounds. Now, she sold her skills to those who could afford them—mercenaries, scholars, even rebels.

Sifraan scanned the ruins, his hand resting on the hilt of his sword. "The scroll's been moved," he muttered.

Samira crouched near the altar, running her fingers over the stone. "Someone was here hours ago. Dust hasn't settled. They took something important."

Kyra tensed, clutching the scroll tighter beneath her cloak.

Aryanath weighed their options. Confrontation was inevitable, but Sifraan's ruthlessness was unpredictable. He motioned to Kyra, signaling for a silent flank.

But Kyra, driven by instinct, moved first. She stepped from the shadows, blade drawn. "You're on sacred ground," she called out.

Sifraan spun, sword flashing in the fading light. "And you carry what we seek."

Before he could advance, Aryanath emerged, his sword raised, its metal catching the last light of the sun. The clash was swift— Sifraan's strikes were heavy, meant to overwhelm, but Aryanath's precision balanced the brute force.

Kyra circled Samira, who wielded twin daggers with the grace of someone used to cutting through the desert winds. Their blades danced in sharp arcs, dust swirling beneath their feet.

"You don't understand what you're carrying," Samira hissed between strikes.

Kyra deflected a blow. "Enlighten me."

Samira's dagger caught Kyra's sleeve, slicing the fabric but missing flesh. "The shattered oath... it wasn't just about protecting knowledge. It was about controlling it. That scroll—people will kill for it."

Kyra's next strike knocked the dagger from Samira's hand, sending it clattering across the stones. "And what makes you different?"

Before Samira could answer, Aryanath forced Sifraan back against the altar, the rogue's blade skidding from his grasp. Dust settled around them as the tension finally broke.

Sifraan, pinned beneath Aryanath's sword, grinned. "You think this ends with us? There are more coming. The past won't stay buried for long."

Aryanath didn't flinch. "We're counting on it."

With a quick motion, Kyra disarmed Samira completely, who raised her hands in surrender.

"Leave," Aryanath ordered. "And take your warnings with you."

Sifraan sneered but retreated, pulling Samira along.

As their figures disappeared into the shadows, Kyra exhaled deeply. "We're not the only ones chasing ghosts."

Aryanath glanced at the open sky, where dark clouds gathered in the distance. "No. But we're the only ones who care about what they leave behind."

They left the vihara behind, the weight of the scroll heavier than before—not just because of the knowledge it held, but because of the dangerous eyes now watching.

And the broken oath that had started it all? It was far from forgotten.

Chapter 4: The Silk Route

"The shattered oath... it wasn't just about protecting knowledge. It was about controlling it. That scroll—people will kill for it."

The words lingered in the air like the dust kicked up by passing caravans. The dimly lit chamber smelled of old parchment and damp stone. The flickering light from the oil lamp cast long shadows against the uneven walls, where inscriptions of an older time had begun to fade. Outside, the distant echoes of hooves and muffled voices signaled the pulse of the Silk Route—Kandahar's lifeline, and its greatest curse.

The Silk Route had always been more than a trade path. It was a shifting artery of power, carrying not just silk and spices but secrets, knowledge, and the ambitions of those who sought to rule. Kandahar, nestled between empires, had become a key junction. Here, Persian traders met Indian merchants, Arab scholars exchanged philosophies with Buddhist monks, and warriors disguised as traders assessed the land they hoped to claim.

Kyra stood near the wooden table, her fingers lightly grazing the edge of an ancient scroll. Its seal had been broken long ago, but its weight had not lessened. The script detailed something far more valuable than gold—records of treaties, betrayals, and the hidden knowledge passed through generations. To own it was to control the history of those who sought to shape the world.

Aryanath's eyes remained fixed on the document. "If this falls into the wrong hands, Kandahar will become more than just a battleground—it will be rewritten."

A voice echoed from the archway. "And who decides whose hands are the wrong ones?"

Aryanath turned sharply. Sifraan stood at the threshold, his expression unreadable. Samira followed a step behind him, her gaze flickering over the room as if assessing every exit. They were both supposed to have left. To disappear, just as they always did when the shadows grew too long.

Kyra crossed her arms. "I thought you wanted nothing to do with this anymore."

Sifraan exhaled, stepping inside. "I did. But then I saw what's coming." He walked to the table, his fingers tracing the parchment. "You think this is about protecting knowledge? It never was. It's about who wields it. That scroll—people will kill for it."

Aryanath exchanged a glance with Kyra. They knew Sifraan too well. He wasn't someone who risked himself for lost causes. If he was here, it meant the stakes had changed.

Samira leaned against the wall, her voice calm yet firm. "The Silk Route is no longer just a trade passage. It's a battlefield waiting to erupt. Merchants are carrying more than just silk and spices—they're transporting weapons, forged alliances, and whispers of war. The scroll is just a piece of the puzzle, but whoever controls it... they control history."

Aryanath studied them both for a long moment. He had no reason to trust Sifraan—yet he always did.

Kyra broke the silence. "Then we move together. No more hidden paths. No more half-measures."

Sifraan smirked. "I never liked half-measures anyway."

A sudden commotion outside drew their attention. The rhythmic march of boots signaled an arrival—merchants, perhaps, or something more dangerous. Aryanath moved swiftly to douse the lamp, plunging the chamber into darkness. From the narrow slits in the wooden walls, they watched as a caravan halted outside the temple gates.

Men dismounted, their robes marked with insignias of distant lands. One of them, a figure draped in crimson and gold, scanned the surroundings with a gaze that spoke of silent authority. The Silk Route was often seen as a passage for trade, but these men were no merchants. They carried no silks, no fragrant spices—only swords wrapped in cloth and crates heavy with something unseen.

Kyra's breath slowed. "They're looking for it."

Aryanath nodded. "Then we must move before they do."

The Silk Route had shaped dynasties and shattered empires. Now, it would decide the fate of Kandahar.

The oath had been shattered once. They could not allow it to be rewritten.

Chapter 5: Whispers in the Sand

The night carried a stillness that only the desert knew—an eerie, suffocating silence, broken only by the distant murmur of caravan wheels and the occasional cry of a restless horse. The Silk Route, usually alive with merchants and travelers, had taken on a different presence tonight. Shadows moved with purpose, and the air carried something heavier than dust—secrets.

Aryanath, Kyra, Sifraan, and Samira remained hidden within the temple ruins, their eyes fixed on the figures outside. The caravan that had halted by the gates was no ordinary trade party. Even from a distance, Aryanath recognized the way these men carried themselves—rigid, disciplined, their hands resting too naturally on the hilts of concealed blades.

"Who do you think they are?" Kyra whispered, barely moving her lips.

Sifraan's sharp gaze followed the movements of the man in crimson and gold, the one who had stepped forward from the group. His presence alone commanded attention. The others moved around him like an unspoken hierarchy had already been established.

"He's not a merchant," Sifraan murmured. "Not even close."

Samira inhaled slowly. "Look at the crates they unloaded. The weight, the way they're handling them—those aren't fabrics or spices. Those are weapons."

A heavy realization settled between them. The Silk Route had always been a means of trade, but it had also been a silent warfront for those who understood its true value. The scroll they sought to protect was not just a relic of knowledge—it was a key. A weapon in its own right.

"Do we engage?" Aryanath asked, his hand resting on the hilt of his blade.

Kyra shook her head. "Not yet. We don't know enough. If we strike now, we might destroy any chance of understanding their real purpose."

Sifraan's expression darkened. "Or we might be letting them move closer to what they came for."

Below them, the man in crimson stepped forward. His voice was calm, yet it carried the weight of someone used to being obeyed. "The knowledge we seek is not lost. It is only hidden. And those who hide it will answer to us."

A slow, deliberate silence followed his words. Then, one of his men stepped forward, holding a scroll—an older one, yellowed at the edges but still intact. He unrolled it, revealing a map.

Kyra's breath caught in her throat. She recognized that outline. It was a map of Kandahar's underground passageways.

The temple. The vaults. The routes meant to remain unknown.

Aryanath clenched his fists. "They already know where to look."

A decision had to be made. They couldn't afford to wait any longer.

Sifraan's voice was low, almost too calm. "If they reach the vault before us, this is over."

Kyra looked at him, then at Samira, who was already tightening the cloth around her wrists, preparing for what was coming. The wind carried the sound of the caravan guards shifting their stance, preparing to move.

No more waiting.

Kyra exhaled. "Then we get there first."

The night was about to be shattered.

Chapter 6: The Chase Beneath the Earth

The wind howled through the abandoned ruins, kicking up dust that clung to their skin like a second layer. The moment Kyra uttered the words, "Then we get there first," the group moved as one. There was no hesitation—only the understanding that time was slipping through their fingers like desert sand.

Sifraan was the first to break into motion, his steps swift and silent as he led the way toward a narrow passage hidden beneath layers of rubble. It had once been part of an ancient escape tunnel, buried and forgotten over the years. But now, it was their only chance.

Samira pulled a rusted torch from the wall and struck flint against stone, lighting their path with a weak flickering glow. The passage was damp, the air thick with the scent of old earth and forgotten history.

"This tunnel connects to the underground chamber beneath the temple," Sifraan whispered. "If they follow the map, they'll go through the main entrance. We'll take the hidden route and cut them off."

Aryanath nodded, his jaw tense. "And if they get there before us?"

"Then we'll make sure they regret it."

They moved quickly, the walls around them narrowing as they descended deeper. The weight of centuries pressed down on them—the silence of a past long buried, waiting to be unearthed.

Kyra's fingers trailed against the carvings on the walls, ancient inscriptions of a time when knowledge was guarded like a sacred flame. This place had been a refuge, a sanctum for those who dedicated their lives to the pursuit of wisdom. And now, it was at risk of falling into the wrong hands.

A distant noise echoed through the tunnel—the unmistakable sound of boots against stone.

"They're here." Samira's voice was tight, her grip tightening around the dagger at her hip.

Sifraan gestured for them to move faster. "They're using the eastern entrance. If we take the next turn, we can intercept them before they reach the vault."

Aryanath turned sharply at the corner, his heart pounding as he caught sight of a faint light ahead. It was dim, flickering—a torch held by someone just beyond the bend. They were close. Too close.

The moment stretched thin as they approached, every step calculated. Then—

A sudden clang.

The tunnel erupted in chaos as a sword swung from the darkness. Aryanath barely had time to react, his blade clashing against steel as he blocked the attack. Sparks flew in the confined space, illuminating the face of the attacker—one of the crimson-clad men from the caravan.

The battle began in an instant.

Kyra lunged, using the tight space to her advantage as she struck low, forcing another opponent off balance. Samira was quick, her dagger flashing as she moved with precision, a shadow among shadows.

Sifraan engaged the leader—the man in crimson. Their blades met in a flurry of strikes, the clash of metal reverberating through the passage. He was fast, calculated, his movements those of a seasoned fighter.

But Sifraan was just as relentless, his determination forged through years of survival.

The air was thick with dust and sweat, the only sounds the labored breaths and the deadly rhythm of battle.

Then—a shift.

The enemy had reinforcements. More figures flooded the tunnel, and suddenly, the odds turned against them.

"We need to move!" Aryanath shouted, knocking his opponent back with a forceful strike.

Kyra's gaze darted toward a narrow gap in the stone wall—a secondary route. Their only chance.

"Through here!" she called, already moving.

One by one, they followed, disappearing into the darkness just as more enemy swords carved through the air. The passage was tight, forcing them to squeeze through, but they emerged into a wider underground chamber.

The vault.

Columns lined the space, their bases cracked with age. At the centre stood an ancient pedestal, and atop it—the scroll.

Time slowed.

It was within reach. But so were the enemy.

Sifraan wiped the sweat from his brow. "No more running."

Aryanath gripped his sword. "Agreed."

Kyra stepped forward, her stance unwavering. The real battle was about to begin.

Chapter 7: Blades in the Dark

The air inside the underground vault was thick with dust, stirred by the hurried movements of Aryanath and his companions. The scroll rested atop the stone pedestal, illuminated by the dim torchlight, its edges curled with age. It was within reach. But so were their enemies.

The men in crimson—mercenaries, assassins, or something worse—emerged from the tunnel like shadows spilling into the chamber. Their leader, a towering figure with a scar running down his jaw, stepped forward, the gleam of his sword catching the torchlight.

"You've led us straight to it," he said, his voice a gravelly rasp. "How convenient."

Aryanath tightened his grip on his blade. "You won't leave with it."

The man smirked. "Neither will you."

Then the fight began.

The chamber erupted in chaos as swords met with a clash of steel. Aryanath blocked the first strike with a sharp parry, redirecting the mercenary's blade before countering with a swift cut to the man's shoulder. Blood spattered against the stone floor, but the enemy barely flinched.

To his left, Kyra moved like a storm. She ducked under a wild swing, pivoting with precision before slashing upward, her blade slicing through leather armour. Her opponent staggered back, but another took his place almost immediately.

Samira, quick and ruthless, slipped between the fighters, her dagger flashing as she found the gaps in their defences. A sharp cry rang out as she drove her blade between an enemy's ribs, yanking it free just in time to parry another attack.

Sifraan's battle was brutal. His opponent was no ordinary swordsman—he was trained, skilled, relentless. Their blades clashed in rapid succession, each strike met with equal force. The mercenary was strong, but Sifraan was faster. He ducked low, sweeping his leg beneath the man's stance, sending him crashing to the ground. Before the enemy could rise, Sifraan drove his sword through his chest.

The battle raged, but more mercenaries poured in.

"We can't hold this position forever!" Kyra shouted, her breath ragged as she dodged another blow.

Aryanath spotted their only chance. A section of the chamber's stone wall had cracked over time, revealing a narrow passage behind it. If they could reach it, they could escape—but not without the scroll.

Sifraan understood his glance immediately. "Cover me," he growled, rushing toward the pedestal.

The leader of the mercenaries saw his intent and moved to intercept. But Aryanath was faster. He lunged, meeting the enemy head-on. Their swords crashed together in a furious exchange of strikes, sparks flying as metal bit against metal.

"You don't even know what you're protecting," the man sneered, locking blades with Aryanath.

Aryanath forced him back, muscles straining. "I know enough."

Sifraan reached the pedestal. His fingers closed around the scroll.

The mercenary leader's eyes widened. "STOP HIM!"

Too late.

Sifraan yanked the scroll free, spinning on his heel just as another enemy lunged. He ducked, narrowly avoiding the sword aimed for his neck, then drove his dagger into the attacker's thigh.

"We have it!" he shouted.

Samira had already cleared a path to the narrow passage. "Go—NOW!"

Aryanath and Kyra fell back, parrying attacks as they retreated. The mercenaries swarmed forward, relentless. One nearly reached Kyra—but she spun at the last second, slashing her blade across his chest.

Samira was the first through the passage, followed by Kyra. Sifraan shoved Aryanath ahead before turning back one last time, meeting the gaze of the mercenary leader.

"This isn't over," the man promised, blood trickling from a cut on his brow.

Sifraan smirked. "I know."

Then he disappeared into the passage.

The last thing Aryanath saw before the tunnel curved into darkness was the mercenaries closing in on the empty pedestal—realising they had failed.

Chapter 8: Ties Forged in Fire

The passage was narrow, the jagged stone walls scraping against their shoulders as they moved through the dimly lit tunnel. Behind them, the muffled shouts of the mercenaries faded, swallowed by the depths of the underground labyrinth. The tension in the air was palpable, but they had the scroll.

As the adrenaline of battle ebbed, the silence grew heavier. The only sounds were their hurried footsteps and the distant drip of water echoing through the tunnels.

Aryanath led the way, fingers brushing against the damp walls, guiding them forward. Kyra followed closely, her breath still uneven from the fight. Samira and Sifraan, though moving with the group, exchanged glances—silent words only they understood.

It was Kyra who finally broke the quiet. "How did you two meet?"

A pause. Then Sifraan exhaled a quiet laugh. "Balkh."

Years Ago – The Streets of Balkh

Balkh was a city of contradiction—wealthy yet ruthless, where scholars and merchants thrived, but so did thieves and assassins. It wasn't a place for the weak.

Samira had learned early how to disappear in its chaos. She knew which streets swallowed men whole, which shadows carried knives. But that night, she had been watched.

The rain had turned the dirt paths slick, and the scent of damp spice lingered in the air. She had just lifted a pouch of coins from an unsuspecting merchant when she felt it— a presence.

Turning sharply, she met his gaze.

Sifraan.

He wasn't like the others—no heavy cloak, no crude threats. He stood with the ease of someone who knew the city's undercurrents, his arms crossed, a hint of amusement in his eyes.

"You're good," he had said. "But you're predictable."

Samira's fingers brushed the hilt of her dagger. "And you are?"

Sifraan flipped a coin in the air, catching it without looking. "Someone who knows talent when he sees it."

She didn't trust easy compliments. In Balkh, they were often the start of a trap. But Sifraan never made an offer—not then.

Instead, fate did its work.

A skirmish in the marketplace. Chaos neither of them saw coming. And a choice — stand alone, or fight together.

The market had been alive with the scent of roasted almonds, saffron, and the sweat of traders haggling over silks and spices.

Merchants called out their wares, their voices overlapping in a symphony of commerce, while beggars wove through the crowd, hands outstretched.

Samira had been watching from the shadows, her sharp eyes locked on the exchange between a Persian moneylender and a burly trader draped in embroidered wool. A purse, heavy with gold, exchanged hands. The moment the coins disappeared into the folds of the trader's sash, she made her move.

Her fingers were swift, practiced. In a single motion, she had the pouch and was already blending into the flow of bodies. But the trader was quicker than she expected.

A shout.

A hand grabbed her wrist.

The next thing she knew, three men—mercenaries, armed with curved daggers—had encircled her, their expressions sharp with amusement.

"She's got nerve," one of them sneered, rolling his blade between his fingers.

Samira had been in tight spots before, but something about these men sent a shiver down her spine. They weren't ordinary guards.

And that was when Sifraan appeared.

He moved like a shadow through the crowd, cutting through the chaos like he had always belonged to it. He didn't hesitate. A flick of his wrist, and a small dagger sank into the arm of the man closest to Samira.

The mercenary let out a strangled grunt as he staggered backward.

For a second, the world held its breath.

Then, chaos erupted.

The remaining two lunged. Samira ducked under the first swing, rolling across the dusty ground as a blade narrowly missed her ribs. Sifraan caught the other attacker by the wrist, twisting sharply until the knife clattered onto the stone. A solid punch sent the man reeling.

The market had dissolved into a frenzy—traders scrambling to save their wares, bystanders shouting, coins spilling across the ground.

She could run.

Escape.

But then she saw Sifraan, now fending off both mercenaries at once, his movements calculated yet reckless.

A choice lay before her.

Stand alone, or fight together.

Her hesitation lasted only a breath.

She grabbed the fallen knife, spun on her heel, and drove it into the shoulder of the closest mercenary.

Sifraan smirked.

They had chosen.

Samira exhaled, shaking herself from the memory. "Sifraan saved my life once."

Sifraan smirked. "And you've been keeping count ever since?"

She rolled her eyes. "Hardly."

Aryanath listened in silence. He had seen many warriors fight side by side, but few with a bond like theirs—seamless, unspoken, unyielding.

Kyra tilted her head. "And what keeps you together now?"

For once, Sifraan didn't answer immediately. He glanced at Samira, something unspoken passing between them.

Finally, he said, "Some bonds aren't made by blood. They're forged in fire."

Samira smirked. "And once forged, they don't break."

The tunnel ahead widened, revealing the first slivers of moonlight filtering through a crack in the stone.

Their journey wasn't over.

But their past had shaped them. And their bond—like tempered steel—was unbreakable.

Chapter 9: The Ties That Bind

The winter air carried a sharp chill, curling through the towering mimosa trees that lined the path to the ancient temple. Aryanath walked ahead, his breath rising in faint clouds, his steps steady yet cautious. Behind him, Kyra moved with silent grace, her deep blue cloak blending with the shadows of the trees. The temple they approached was nothing more than a forgotten ruin to most, but to them, it was something more—something waiting to be uncovered.

Two years before fate would place Darius in Kyra's life, she and Aryanath had only ever known each other as constants. They had been together since they were children, two souls shaped by the same fires of knowledge and discipline. He had been her shadow when she wandered too far from the palace gardens, and she had been his voice of reason when his anger threatened to consume him. Though no words had ever named what they were to each other, something unspoken always tethered them together.

Kyra's gaze fell upon Aryanath's back as he studied the temple entrance. Even as a child, he had been drawn to places like this—ancient, mysterious, and forgotten. It had been Aryanath who first led her into the depths of old scriptures and temple archives, his thirst for knowledge matching her own. And now, at eighteen, they stood at the threshold of something far greater than either of them could have foreseen.

"This place," Kyra murmured, running her gloved fingers over the weathered stone. "It was meant to be found."

Aryanath glanced at her, his dark eyes unreadable. "Then it's a good thing we're here."

Sifraan and Samira joined them at the steps. The bond between them mirrored Kyra and Aryanath's—wordless, yet unbreakable. Sifraan, ever watchful, rested his hand on the hilt of his blade, while Samira's sharp gaze scanned the treetops, ensuring they weren't being followed.

Inside, the temple was a hushed expanse of cold stone and forgotten history. In its heart, they discovered an underground chamber lined with carvings and inscriptions—the Chamber of Commerce, a relic of a time when trade had flourished through Kandahar's corridors.

Aryanath's fingers traced the inscriptions, his mind racing with the implications of what they had found. This temple, abandoned now, would one day become something far greater. He could see it in his mind—fortresses rising, the walls reinforced, the chamber at the center of something grand.

Kyra, standing beside him, seemed to see it too.

"Someone will come," she said softly. "Someone will build upon this."

And she was right. Years from now, Darius would fortify these ruins into an unyielding stronghold. The pieces of the story were falling into place, and Aryanath was the one who held them together.

But the past had a way of demanding its due. And outside, in the whispering dark, danger lurked. The man in the red and gold robe had finally caught up to them.

The night would not end without blood.

Chapter 10: The Warrior's Farewell

The cold air thickened with the scent of damp earth and smoke. Night had fallen over the temple ruins, the moon casting jagged shadows through the gaps in the ancient stone. The silence was deceptive—too still, too expectant.

Aryanath knew before he even turned. A presence in the darkness, measured steps against the uneven ground. Then—gold gleaming in the firelight.

The man in the red and gold robe had found them.

Sifraan was the first to draw his blade. "Run," he murmured, barely audible.

Kyra didn't move. Neither did Samira.

They had come too far to run.

The man in the robe stepped forward, his face shrouded in the flickering torchlight. He did not come alone. Shadows moved behind him—figures armed, waiting for a command.

"You shouldn't have come here," the man said. His voice was smooth, almost amused. "This place does not belong to you."

Aryanath stepped forward, his own blade unsheathed. "And it belongs to you?"

A low chuckle. "It belongs to those who understand its value."

Sifraan moved first. A blade cut through the air, but the man in the robe was faster. Steel met steel, sparks flying as their swords clashed.

Then chaos erupted.

The enemy soldiers lunged, and the temple grounds became a battlefield.

Aryanath fought with precision, his movements honed from years of training. He saw Kyra beside him, her dagger a blur, striking where it mattered. Samira, fierce and relentless, held her ground against two men at once.

Sifraan had engaged the leader, their fight a brutal display of strength and strategy.

Every strike was met with an equal counter, neither yielding.

Until the mistake.

A sudden misstep. A shift in weight.

And the blade drove deep into Sifraan's chest.

Time seemed to slow.

Samira screamed his name, but he only stumbled, his grip on his sword loosening. He turned—his eyes meeting Aryanath's. There was no fear in them, only understanding.

Then he fell.

Samira was there in an instant, cradling him as blood soaked the earth. Her hands trembled, pressing against the wound as if she could will it closed.

"No," she whispered. "No, no, no—"

Sifraan exhaled shakily, his hand reaching for Samira. His fingers barely brushed against his friend's wrist before they slackened. His gaze lingered, a silent farewell.

And then he was gone.

Aryanath's grip tightened around his sword. His heart pounded, a storm of rage and grief.

The man in the red and gold robe turned toward him, wiping the blood from his blade. "A waste," he murmured. "He could have—"

He never finished his sentence.

Aryanath moved like lightning, fury igniting every muscle. His sword found its mark, slicing through flesh, bone, purpose.

The leader's eyes widened in shock as he staggered, gasping. A single moment, then he collapsed, his robe pooling around him like spilled wine.

Silence returned.

But it was different now. Heavier.

Samira's sobs broke through the quiet, her fingers still tangled in Sifraan's hair. Kyra knelt beside her, her own face pale with grief.

Aryanath turned away, his hands shaking. Revenge had come swiftly, but it brought no solace.

The last look in Sifraan's eyes would never leave him.

Chapter 11: Warriors and Scholars

The morning was heavy with silence. The cold earth, damp from the night's rain, clung to their hands as they dug the grave beneath the shade of the ancient mimosa trees. The golden hues of dawn filtered through the leaves, casting long shadows over Sifraan's still body.

Aryanath knelt beside him, his hands coated in dirt and blood. His face was unreadable, but his shoulders carried the weight of the night before. Kyra stood beside him, her blue cloak wrapped tightly around her as if shielding herself from the loss that had settled deep within her chest.

Samira had not spoken since the moment Sifraan had drawn his last breath. She knelt beside him now, her fingers tracing the edge of the amulet he had always worn around his neck. Her eyes, once sharp and full of mischief, were hollow.

The burial was not rushed. It was a warrior's farewell. They laid Sifraan to rest with his sword across his chest, his scabbard at his side. Kyra placed a single relic beside him—a carved stone that had once been part of the temple walls. A symbol of what he had fought for.

As the last handful of soil fell upon the grave, Aryanath stood. His fists clenched, his knuckles white. "He should have lived," he murmured, voice rough.

"He did," Kyra whispered, placing a hand on his arm. "And he will."

They stood in silence, each carrying their grief in their own way.

The land that once stretched far beyond the mountains, ruled by Kyra's ancestors, had begun to disintegrate. Where once there had been unity, now there were factions—small rulers vying for control, alliances shifting like sand in the wind.

With the weakening of the central authority, the temple that had once been a beacon of knowledge and power was now under constant threat. The hidden relics—scrolls, artefacts, scriptures that held the weight of history—were no longer safe. They had to be retrieved before they fell into enemy hands.

It was why Aryanath and Kyra had ventured so deep into the forgotten chambers of the temple. Why they had risked their lives to reclaim what had been lost.

Now, as they made their way back to their community, their hands bore more than just the weight of their weapons. They carried knowledge—the very thing their enemies sought to destroy.

The Scholars of Kandahar

The village was waiting for them. Elders, warriors, children—they all stood as Aryanath and Kyra approached, their cloaks torn, their faces lined with exhaustion. But their hands were full. The ancient scrolls, the relics, the knowledge that had been buried beneath the temple's ruins—it was all here.

Bhadrasen, the wisest among them, stepped forward. His eyes, aged and knowing, moved between Kyra and Aryanath. "You have done what no one before you could," he said, his voice heavy with pride. "You have brought back what was lost."

The people murmured, heads bowing in quiet respect.

Bhadrasen lifted his hand, and the crowd fell silent. "From this day forth, you are no longer just warriors. You are the Scholars of Kandahar—keepers of its past, protectors of its future."

The words settled over them like the weight of destiny. Kyra met Aryanath's gaze, and in that moment, she understood. This had always been their path.

Rajvanta, the commander of their army, stepped forward next. He turned to Samira, whose grief had not yet faded, but whose resolve had sharpened.

"You fought for Sifraan," Rajvanta said. "You fought for us all." His voice was steady. "From this day on, you will be the Chief Spy of our people."

Samira blinked, her breath catching. She had lost so much. But now, she had a purpose.

The community erupted in murmurs of approval. A new era had begun.

Kyra clenched her fists, her heart steady. The past had brought them here. But the future? That was theirs to shape.

Chapter 12: The Unfinished Prophecy

The night was thick with whispers, the air heavy with the scent of burning oil lamps and the distant murmurs of a world that did not sleep. The Chamber of Commerce lay behind them now, but the weight of its secrets still clung to their skins like the dust of its ancient walls. Kyra walked ahead, her mind a storm of thoughts, her fingers still tingling from the relics they had retrieved.

Beside her, Aryanath moved like a shadow, his presence a constant reminder of the bond they had shared since childhood. Yet tonight, something had shifted. The grief of losing Sifraan had settled in, but more than that, the unspoken tension between them was thick enough to drown in.

Ahead, the path twisted into the heart of the kingdom—a kingdom that had once been ruled by Kyra's ancestors but was now crumbling under the weight of shifting power. The relics they carried held more than history; they held the last threads of control that could either bind them to the past or break them free.

But they weren't the only ones who knew of their existence.

The Stranger in the Shadows

As they neared the main square, a figure stepped out from the veil of night. Clad in deep indigo robes, his presence was as silent as the desert winds, yet his gaze held the weight of someone who had been watching for far too long.

Aryanath's hand hovered over the hilt of his blade. Kyra, however, held up a hand— an instinct she couldn't explain.

The man lowered his hood, revealing sharp, angular features and piercing dark eyes. "You carry something that does not belong to you," he said in a voice that was both smooth and dangerous.

Aryanath took a step forward, his stance rigid. "And who are you to decide that?"

The stranger smiled, slow and deliberate. "A man who knows the cost of forgotten history."

Kyra felt a flicker of recognition, though she was certain she had never seen him before. But there was something about his presence—something unsettling yet familiar.

"We are not here for a trade," she said evenly. "The relics belong to this land, to its people."

The man tilted his head. "And yet, history tells us that power never remains in one place for long." His gaze lingered on Kyra. "Especially when fate intervenes."

Aryanath's jaw tightened. "Who sent you?"

The stranger did not answer. Instead, he stepped back into the darkness, his parting words curling around them like smoke.

"Be careful what you seek. Some prophecies are better left unfinished."

Then, he was gone.

They reached the temple's outer sanctum, where the elders of the community waited. The moment Kyra and Aryanath placed the relics before them, murmurs filled the air. The scrolls were untouched by time, their words weaving a tale of lost power, hidden betrayals, and a destiny that had yet to be fulfilled.

Bhadrasen, the elder who had watched them grow from reckless children into warriors, stood. His gaze was unreadable as he looked at Kyra. "You have done what many before you could not."

Kyra's throat tightened, the weight of expectation settling on her shoulders.

Rajvanta, the army commander, stepped forward. "From this night forward, you are no longer just seekers of knowledge. You are its protectors."

The words settled deep within her bones.

Aryanath turned to her, something unreadable in his expression. There was pride, yes, but there was also something else—a hesitation, a knowing.

Because the truth was, they had always been bound together by something greater than titles or duty.

And yet, destiny had its own plans.

Later that night, as the torches burned low and the world outside quieted, Kyra found herself standing alone beneath the mimosa trees. The scent of their golden blooms filled the air, their branches swaying with the night wind.

Footsteps approached—silent, yet known to her.

She didn't have to turn to know it was Aryanath.

For a long moment, neither of them spoke. But when she finally turned, she found his gaze locked on hers, something burning beneath the surface.

"This path we walk..." his voice was low, edged with something raw, "it has always been ours, hasn't it?"

Kyra's breath caught. Because she knew what he meant. What he had always meant.

Their bond had never needed words, yet it was the one thing that had remained unshaken through war, through loss, through the shifting sands of fate.

Yet, for the first time, Kyra wasn't sure if destiny was their ally—or their enemy.

But tonight, as Aryanath reached for her hand, fingers brushing against hers with a warmth that set her pulse racing, she chose to forget the future.

Tonight, they were just two souls bound by something neither of them could explain.

And in the silence between them,
something unspoken was set aflame.

Chapter 13: The Shadows Between Us

A restless wind carried the scent of damp earth and mimosa blossoms through the temple grounds. The air was thick with the weight of the past, pressing against Kyra's chest like an unseen force.

She stood near the temple wall, her gaze fixed on the horizon where storm clouds gathered, dark and heavy. Somewhere beyond those clouds, destiny moved like an unseen thread, pulling them toward something inevitable.

"You should be resting," Aryanath's voice broke through the silence.

Kyra didn't turn. "So should you."

He came to stand beside her, the quiet tension between them more familiar than words. His presence had always been constant—since childhood, since they had first been bound by the invisible thread of fate.

But fate had a cruel way of testing them.

"You haven't been yourself," Aryanath said, studying her.

Kyra's fingers brushed the stone of the temple wall. She hesitated before speaking.

"The stranger! He knew about the relics."

Aryanath's expression darkened. "And?"

"And he knew about us."

A heavy silence settled between them. She had kept the encounter to herself, unsure of what to make of it, but now, as pieces of a larger scheme began to fall into place, she could no longer ignore the feeling clawing at her chest.

He looked at her, and for a moment, everything else faded. The temple, the prophecy, the war looming at their backs—it all became distant compared to the weight of the look in his eyes.

A silence stretched between them, filled with something unspoken, something neither of them dared to name.

Before Aryanath could respond, the night shifted.

A shadow moved at the temple's edge.

Kyra tensed. Aryanath's hand went to his sword.

A voice, smooth and taunting, drifted from the darkness.

"How poetic," the stranger from the square stepped forward, his smirk illuminated by the moonlight. "A princess and her protector, standing on the edge of history."

A Trap Unfolds

Kyra's fingers tightened around the dagger at her waist. She recognized the men flanking him—mercenaries, blades drawn, eyes glinting with something far worse than greed.

"You took something that does not belong to you," the stranger continued. "And now, we've come to take it back."

Aryanath's stance shifted, poised for a fight. "Try."

The mercenaries surged forward.

Kyra sidestepped an attack, driving her dagger into the attacker's arm before twisting away. Aryanath met the first strike head-on, his sword a flash of steel against the night.

Kyra moved in the same breath, twisting away from a dagger aimed at her ribs. She grabbed the man's wrist, using his own momentum to flip him onto his back before driving her knee into his chest.

Another attacker came from behind. She spun, ducking beneath a wild swing before striking out with her elbow, catching him hard across the jaw.

Aryanath was a storm beside her, his movements fluid, relentless. He disarmed one of the men with ease, twisting the blade from his grip before driving his sword through his shoulder.

But there were too many.

And the stranger was just standing there, watching.

A figure moved behind Aryanath, blade poised for a fatal strike. Kyra saw it a second too late.

She threw herself forward.

Pain exploded through her shoulder as the dagger meant for Aryanath buried itself in her flesh instead.

Aryanath's roar of fury barely reached her ears before the darkness closed in.

Kyra's first sensation was warmth—Aryanath's hand gripping hers. Then pain, sharp and deep, as she forced her eyes open.

"You should have let me handle it," Aryanath's voice was low, raw.

She exhaled a weak laugh. "You would have done the same."

His jaw clenched.

The stranger was gone. But his message lingered.

Kyra forced herself upright, despite the burning in her shoulder. "This isn't over."

Aryanath didn't let go of her hand.

"No," he agreed.

The battle was far from over.

Kyra reached up, gripping Aryanath's wrist. "We need to end this."

His fingers curled over hers, firm, steady.

"We will," he promised.

And this time, she believed him.

Chapter 14: The Reckoning

The temple courtyard lay in uneasy silence, broken only by the rustling of mimosa leaves in the cold night wind. The weight of failure pressed against Kyra's chest, as heavy as the bloodied bandages on her shoulder. The scroll—the key to everything—was gone.

Stolen by the man in the indigo robe.

Aryanath stood a few paces away, his jaw tight, his knuckles white around the hilt of his sword. His silence was louder than any words.

"They planned this," Kyra finally said, her voice barely above a whisper. "They knew exactly when to strike."

Aryanath didn't respond immediately. His gaze was fixed on the dark horizon, where the man in indigo had vanished into the night.

"He underestimated us," Aryanath said at last. His voice was calm, but there was a dangerous edge beneath it. "And that was his first mistake."

Kyra met his eyes. "Then let's make sure he doesn't get a second."

Before the plan was set into motion, Samira uncovered the whereabouts of the man in the indigo robe. Disguised as a wandering merchant, she had slipped into the underbelly of the city, listening to whispers in the shadowed corners of taverns and trading posts. It was in a dimly lit house, hidden within the maze of the old marketplace, that she overheard a group of mercenaries speaking in hushed tones about their employer—a man draped in indigo, who had taken refuge in the abandoned caravanserai by the river. Samira had followed them, moving like a ghost through the crowded streets, until she caught sight of the man himself disappearing behind the crumbling walls of his temporary stronghold.

Without wasting another moment, she returned to the courtroom her breath ragged but her eyes burning with certainty. "I found him," she had said, sealing their course of action with those three simple words.

The Plan

Rajvanta entered the courtyard, his face grim. Behind him stood twelve warriors—men and women from their tribe, hardened by years of war and survival. These were not mercenaries. They were blood-bound to the land, to the temple, to each other. And tonight, they would fight for what was stolen.

"We move at midnight," Aryanath said, his voice cutting through the air like a blade. "The man in indigo has taken refuge in the old caravanserai near the river. It's heavily guarded, but they won't be expecting a full assault."

Rajvanta crossed his arms. "Twelve against an unknown number of fighters?"

Kyra smirked. "We've faced worse odds."

Rajvanta studied her for a moment before nodding. "Then let's make sure we don't waste this opportunity."

They gathered around a rough map drawn in the dirt. Aryanath pointed to the western side of the caravanserai. "Rajvanta, you'll take six men and create a diversion here. Light the supply carts on fire. That should draw most of them out."

Kyra traced a path along the eastern wall. "I'll go in from here with Aryanath and the rest. We take down the remaining guards and get to the scroll before they realize what's happening."

One of the warriors, a scarred man named Beera, grunted. "And the man in indigo?"

Aryanath's eyes darkened. "Leave him to me."

A hush fell over the group. Everyone knew what that meant.

The man in indigo would not be walking out of there alive.

The Infiltration

The moon hung low as they moved through the dense brush, their footfalls swallowed by the earth. The caravanserai loomed ahead, its crumbling walls bathed in torchlight. Figures moved inside—guards, traders, mercenaries.

Kyra pressed a hand to her dagger. "It's now or never."

Rajvanta and his team slipped away first. Moments later, the night erupted with the sound of flames and shouting. Smoke curled into the sky as fire consumed the supply carts.

It was their cue.

Aryanath, Kyra, and the others moved swiftly, scaling the eastern wall. The first guard barely had time to react before Kyra slit his throat, his body crumpling without a sound.

Inside, chaos reigned. The guards were scrambling, drawn to the fire. But not all had left.

A sword came at Aryanath. He dodged, countered, and in one swift motion, drove his blade through his attacker's ribs. Kyra had already taken down another, her dagger slick with blood.

They moved toward the central chamber. And there he was.

The man in indigo.

His back was to them, his hands clasped behind him as he studied the scroll laid out on the table.

But as Aryanath stepped forward, the man turned.

The torches flickered, casting shadows over his face.

Kyra stiffened. His features were unfamiliar—sharp, angular, his dark eyes filled with a quiet arrogance. This was no ordinary thief.

Aryanath exhaled, a single name escaping his lips like a curse.

"Ziaqat."

Kyra's breath caught.

Ziaqat came from a different world, a different clan—immigrants from the far east, men who carried foreign steel and fought for coin, not honour.

And worse, he had served the man who had killed Sifraan.

A slow smirk spread across Ziaqat's face. "I was wondering when you'd come."

The Reckoning

Aryanath lunged.

Ziaqat was fast. He dodged, drawing his own blade. Their swords clashed, ringing through the chamber. Kyra circled, waiting for her moment, her gaze never leaving Ziaqat's every move.

"You should have stayed out of this," Aryanath spat, striking again.

Ziaqat laughed. "And miss this moment? Watching you scramble in the dark for scraps?" He parried the next strike with ease. "The scroll belongs to my master now."

Kyra saw her opening. She moved in, her dagger slashing toward Ziaqat's side. But he was ready.

His elbow shot back, catching her in the ribs. Pain exploded through her, but she didn't falter.

Aryanath pressed forward, his attacks relentless. Steel met steel, sparks flying.

Then, with a sudden shift, Aryanath feinted—leaving Ziaqat open.

Kyra didn't hesitate.

Her dagger plunged into his throat.

Ziaqat gasped, staggering. His eyes met hers, something flickering in them—anger, disbelief...

perhaps regret.

He fell to his knees. Blood pooled beneath him.

Aryanath stepped forward, yanking the dagger free. "This was for Sifraan."

Ziaqat choked on his breath, his smirk faltering. And then he was still.

The room was silent.

The scroll was theirs again.

Kyra exhaled, her hands trembling slightly. Aryanath placed a hand on her shoulder, grounding her.

"It's over," he said.

She met his gaze, her heart still pounding. "Not yet."

Because the war wasn't finished. The enemies wouldn't stop. And the price of this night would come due.

But for now, they had won.

Chapter 15: The Unspoken Promise

The scent of burning oil lamps and damp stone lingered as the group huddled within the temple ruins, their bodies tense with the anticipation of what lay ahead. The stolen scroll had to be retrieved, and the battle was yet to come. But in the flickering glow of the fire, Aryanath's gaze was drawn to Kyra—not as a fellow warrior, nor as the Scholar she was destined to become, but as something more.

She stood apart from the others, arms folded as she examined the old maps laid out before her. The firelight cast shifting shadows over her face, tracing the sharp angles of her jaw and the determined set of her lips. Strands of her dark hair had come loose from her braid, framing her features with an untamed elegance. She was fierce, resolute, unshaken—yet in the quiet moments, when no one was watching, Aryanath caught glimpses of the weight she carried. The burden of legacy. The silent grief for those they had lost. The responsibility that neither of them had asked for but had accepted without hesitation.

Kyra sensed his eyes on her and turned, her gaze meeting his with a question unspoken. "What?" she asked, her voice softer than usual.

Aryanath hesitated, then shook his head with a small smile. "Nothing," he murmured, though the truth sat heavy on his tongue. Nothing—except that he had admired her for as long as he could remember. Nothing—except that, in the chaos of war and duty, she was the one constant he had always held onto.

But there were no words for what lay between them. Not yet.

Instead, he stepped closer, lowering his voice so only she could hear.

"You don't have to bear this alone, Kyra."

She let out a quiet breath, the hardness in her eyes faltering just slightly. "I know," she said.

But Aryanath could see that she didn't.

And in that moment, as the wind rustled through the broken pillars of the temple, carrying whispers of the past and the battles yet to come, he made a silent promise to himself. He would stand by her, no matter what. Even if the world fell apart around them, even if fate pulled them toward different paths—he would never leave her side.

Chapter 16: Beneath the Surface

The chamber was dimly lit by flickering torches, their glow barely reaching the edges of the stone walls. The scent of damp earth mixed with the sharp tang of aged parchment.

On the table between them lay the scroll—the very thing they had risked their lives for. Aryanath and Kyra stared at it in silence, the weight of its contents pressing down on them like an unseen force.

This wasn't just any ancient text. It was a map—a secret guide to the underground pathways of Kandahar, routes hidden beneath the city that connected it to strategically vital locations.

Whoever controlled these tunnels controlled Kandahar.

Aryanath traced a finger over the delicate ink markings. The intricate network of passageways spread like veins, leading to unknown depths. These paths were more than just escape routes; they were the key to victory over any invader. With them, their people could disappear when needed, regroup in safety, and strike from the shadows.

Kyra exhaled slowly. "This is why they wanted it so badly."

Aryanath nodded. "With this, we can outmanoeuvre any enemy. They won't even know where to look."

She looked at him then, something unreadable in her gaze. He knew what she was thinking. For years, they had fought battles in the open, relying on their strength, their numbers. But war wasn't always won by swords alone. Sometimes, the greatest victories were secured in the shadows.

He turned back to the scroll, feeling the tension coil inside him. This knowledge had to be protected at all costs.

But even as the realisation settled, Aryanath's focus shifted—from the parchment to the woman beside him.

Kyra.

She had been his constant, his fiercest ally, the one person he trusted beyond all reason. And yet, in moments like this, when the world was quiet, when there was nothing but the space between them, he felt something deeper, something he had spent years suppressing.

He reached for her hand before he could stop himself. Their fingers barely touched, but it sent a spark through him. Kyra turned to him, her dark eyes searching his face.

And then, without thinking, without hesitation, Aryanath closed the distance between them and kissed her.

The moment was raw, desperate. His lips

moved against hers with years of restraint unraveling at once. She gasped against him but didn't pull away. Instead, she met his urgency with her own, her fingers gripping his tunic.

For that brief, stolen moment, there was no war. No scroll. No looming threats. Just them.

But then, as quickly as it had begun, Kyra pulled away, breathless. "Aryanath..."

She didn't need to say more.

The shouts from outside shattered the silence, pulling them back into reality.

Duty called.

Chapter 17: The boy from Sindh

The night lay thick over Kandahar, a quiet veil of darkness stretching across the city like the hush before a storm. The air smelled of burnt oil and dust, mingling with the lingering scent of jasmine from the temple gardens. Within the stone walls of the temple chamber, Aryanath and Kyra sat in silence, their gazes locked upon the scattered parchments and maps between them.

The flames of the oil lamps flickered, throwing restless shadows across the intricate carvings on the walls—stories of old, of rulers long forgotten, of wars fought and won, of gods watching over mortals who had risen and fallen in their time. Outside, the world was shifting. Empires were crumbling, new powers rising from the ruins of the old. The Abbasid Caliphate, once an unshakable force, was fraying at the edges. To the west, the Saffarids, under the ruthless command of Ya'qub ibn al-Layth, were moving like a tide, swallowing cities and fortresses in their wake.

Kandahar, positioned at the crossroads of great civilizations, was more than just a city. It was a gateway—one that traders, conquerors, and scholars alike had sought to control for centuries. And now, the question loomed: Who would hold Kandahar's fate in their hands?

Kyra shifted slightly, the rich fabric of her robe rustling against the stone floor. "We are standing on the edge of something greater than ourselves, Aryanath," she said, her voice measured but grave. "The world is not what it was five years ago. The trade routes are no longer safe, and the roads are filled with whispers of war. If we do not act, we risk losing everything—not just our people, but the legacy of those who came before us."

Aryanath, his dark eyes shadowed with thought, ran his fingers along the worn edges of an ancient map. "The caravans from Balkh have been intercepted. The last traders who arrived spoke of raids along the roads. If the Saffarids move further east, they will come for us. And if they control the Silk Road, they control the wealth of the region."

His jaw tightened as he looked up at Kyra. "We have always fought for

Kandahar's survival, but this... this is different. If we lose this battle, we lose more than our land. We lose our identity."

Before Kyra could respond, the heavy wooden doors creaked open, the sound echoing through the chamber. A figure stepped inside—a young man, barely sixteen, yet his face bore the weariness of a traveler who had seen too much. He was dressed in dust-streaked robes, his sandals worn from endless miles on the road. His skin was darkened by the sun, and his eyes, sharp and unyielding, held a wisdom far beyond his years.

"I am Kanak," the boy said, his voice steady. "I come from Sindh, but my journey has taken me farther than most men dream."

Kyra and Aryanath exchanged a glance.

Kanak stepped closer and unrolled a delicate scroll, laying it upon the stone floor before them. The parchment was covered in intricate symbols, the script ancient and precise. "This is knowledge from Sharda Peeth," he continued, his voice barely above a whisper. "A centre of learning where scholars from all lands gather. The rulers of the past who understood power knew that true strength does not lie in swords, nor in gold—but in knowledge."

Kyra's breath caught as she traced the symbols with her fingertips. "The wisdom of the ages..." she murmured.

Kanak nodded. "This scroll speaks of empires that rose and fell. It tells of rulers who built their dominions not with brute force, but with understanding—of the land, of trade, of the unseen forces that shape history. The Saffarids, the Abbasids, the traders who walk the Silk Road... they are all playing a game older than time itself."

Aryanath studied the boy carefully. "And where do we fit in this game?"

Kanak met his gaze. "You are not just warriors. You are something more. You are the guardians of a legacy that must not be lost. Kandahar is more than a stronghold—it is a living testament to the past. If it falls, it will not be just another conquest. It will be the loss of centuries of knowledge, of culture, of power that cannot be measured in gold or land."

Kyra turned to Aryanath, her eyes burning with conviction. "Then we must act—not just as soldiers, but as scholars. As protectors."

Aryanath exhaled sharply, his fingers curling into a fist. "The path ahead will demand more from us than we have ever given."

Kanak smiled faintly. "The greatest roads are never easy to walk. But they lead to the future."

A long silence stretched between them as the weight of his words settled into their bones.

Beyond the temple walls, the night deepened, and the wind carried whispers of things yet to come.

For Aryanath and Kyra, the battle for Kandahar's soul was only just beginning.

Chapter 18: The Vanishing Histories

The fire crackled in the dimly lit chamber, casting flickering shadows upon the stone walls. Aryanath and Kyra sat with Kanak, the boy from Sindh, and a handful of their most trusted scholars and warriors. The air was thick with contemplation. Kanak had traveled far, carrying stories of destruction—of invaders who erased histories, not merely by sword, but by silencing the past.

Kyra leaned forward, her piercing gaze fixed on Kanak. "You speak of lost knowledge, of temples and libraries burned to the ground. Tell me, why does an empire seek to erase what was before?"

Kanak, his young face carrying the weight of stories too old for his years, took a deep breath. "Because history holds the power of identity," he replied. "When an invader comes, it is not enough to defeat armies. They must also defeat memories. They erase the teachings, the sacred texts, the stories that define the people, so that those who remain will search endlessly for their roots. A land without history is a land without resistance. It is easier to rule the lost than the rooted."

Aryanath, his jaw clenched, looked at Kyra. "And so they burn the temples, they destroy the pilgrimage sites—not just for faith, but for knowledge. They are not just erasing gods; they are erasing power itself."

Kanak nodded. "Exactly. Take the libraries of Takshashila or Sharda Peeth. These were not just places of learning; they were the heart of civilisation. When they fell, it was not just books that were lost—it was an entire lineage of wisdom, medicine, strategy, and governance. Every time knowledge is destroyed, an empire crumbles, and a new one takes its place. But the cycle repeats. The victors rewrite history to glorify their conquest, and those who come after will never truly know what was lost."

Silence settled over the room. The weight of Kanak's words pressed upon them like an unseen force.

Kyra, her fingers tracing the rim of a copper goblet, spoke softly, "Then how do we break the cycle? How do we ensure that our past does not vanish like the sands of time?"

Aryanath exhaled sharply. "By preserving what we can. By safeguarding what knowledge remains. And by teaching our people that history is not just what is written—it is what is remembered."

Kanak's eyes gleamed. "There are those who still remember. There are hidden places, underground sanctuaries where scrolls and scriptures are kept. But knowledge alone is not enough. The ruling power controls what is taught. If they rewrite history, the people will believe it as truth."

Kyra's heart pounded. She knew Kanak spoke the truth. She had seen how the conquerors who came before had twisted the stories, turning protectors into villains, turning wisdom into myth. "Then we must do more than protect knowledge. We must teach our people to question, to seek beyond what is given to them. We must make sure they know their roots, even if the records are burned."

Aryanath stood, his silhouette tall against the firelight. "And we must fight. Not just with swords, but with truth. If knowledge is the key to power, then we must become the keepers of that power. We must ensure that Kandahar does not forget its own story."

Kanak smiled faintly. "That is why I have come. I have seen what happens when knowledge is lost. But I have also seen what happens when it is protected. There are scrolls, hidden beyond the mountains, in the ruins of old shrines.

They hold secrets—maps, records, teachings that have been passed down for generations. If we can retrieve them, we may yet preserve what is left."

Kyra and Aryanath exchanged a glance. A new mission had begun—not just to fight for their land, but to fight for its history.

The battle for Kandahar was no longer just about warriors and kings. It was a battle for truth itself.

Chapter 19: The Evanescing Ink of Time

The night in Kandahar was heavy with an eerie silence, broken only by the faint rustling of the wind through the ruins of what once were grand centres of learning. Aryanath and Kyra stood by the flickering fire, their expressions dark with contemplation. The weight of history pressed upon them—not just their own, but that of countless civilisations that had risen and fallen before them.

Kanak sat cross-legged beside them, his face illuminated by the firelight, deep in thought. "Every empire that seeks to dominate first turns to erasing the past," he murmured, his voice carrying the wisdom of distant lands. "Destroying knowledge is the surest way to weaken the people. Without roots, a tree withers. Without history, a civilisation forgets itself."

Kyra, still haunted by the remnants of destroyed temples and libraries, nodded solemnly. "The invaders do not merely kill people. They kill memory. They burn scriptures, demolish temples, and silence scholars. In doing so, they erase identities, making it easier to impose their own narratives."

Aryanath's fists clenched. "So they rewrite the future by erasing the past."

Kanak continued, "Look at what happened to Nalanda and Takshashila. The knowledge that once flowed from their walls, shaping generations, was reduced to ashes. The scholars were slaughtered, their wisdom lost, and their people left wandering, unsure of who they once were. It takes centuries to build knowledge, but only moments to destroy it."

Kyra exhaled sharply, looking toward the distant mountains. "And once the conquerors have wiped away the old, they establish their own doctrines, their own truth. A child born after such destruction grows up hearing only what the victors wish them to believe. Soon, even the memory of what was lost fades."

Aryanath's mind was racing. "This is the greatest weapon," he muttered. "Not swords, not armies, but the destruction of knowledge. With no past to anchor them, the people become pawns—easily swayed, easily ruled."

Kanak nodded. "It is why Sharda Peeth was so sacred, why the Vedas were preserved orally for so long—because our ancestors knew that the written word could be burned, but memory, if carried forward, could endure."

A sudden gust of wind sent the fire flickering wildly. Kyra watched the flames dance, their unpredictable movements mirroring the fate of civilisations. "So what do we do?" she asked. "How do we protect knowledge when the world is bent on erasing it?"

Aryanath's gaze met hers, intense and unwavering. "We become the keepers of memory. We learn, we teach, and we ensure that what must not be forgotten is passed down—not through stone and ink, but through the people themselves. So that even if every book burns, the knowledge will still live on."

A newfound resolve settled over them. This was no longer just about protecting Kandahar. It was about safeguarding the very essence of their civilisation. And for that, they needed to act—not with weapons, but with wisdom.

Chapter 20 : The Temple of Asamai

The night air was heavy with the scent of burning oil lamps and the distant hum of conversations from the lower quarters of the city. Aryanath and Kyra sat beneath the open sky, the stars mirroring the embers in their brazier, their weary faces illuminated by the golden flicker of firelight. Kanak, the traveler from Sindh, had brought them knowledge—knowledge that could shift the tides of understanding and power in Kandahar. His voice, smooth yet laced with the weight of history, filled the space between them.

"The Temple of Asamai," Kanak began, adjusting his woollen shawl, "is not just a place of worship. It is a testament to the resilience of time, a beacon that has endured conquests, beliefs, and changing rulers. Its origins are older than many kingdoms that now claim power."

Aryanath leaned forward, intrigued. "Asamai... I have heard of it only in passing, spoken of in reverence. Tell me, Kanak, what do you know of its past?"

Kanak smiled, his face marked by the wisdom of a wanderer who had seen many lands. "Asamai derives its name from the great Asa Mountain, which watches over Kabul. It is a temple of fire, of devotion, and of the eternal spirit. Long before the present rulers, before even the Greeks left their mark upon this land, the sacred flame burned there, unwavering. The followers of the old faith, the Zunbils and the Kushans before them, knew of its significance. The fire within the temple was said to have been kept alight for centuries, tended by priests who believed it to be a bridge between mortals and the divine."

Kyra listened intently, her fingers tracing absent patterns on the stone beside her. "And yet, we barely hear of it now. Why?"

Kanak's expression darkened. "Time erodes not only stone but also memory. When the Arab conquerors took these lands, their banners bringing new faith and order, the temple faced destruction. Yet, the fire never truly died. Some say that the keepers of Asamai carried embers away, ensuring that the sacred light was never lost. Even now, hidden within the hills and among those who remember, the flame flickers in secret."

A gust of wind stirred the fire before them, causing the shadows to dance on the rugged walls of the courtyard. Aryanath exhaled, considering the weight of this revelation. "If the fire still burns, even in hiding, then the temple is not lost."

Kanak nodded. "Indeed. And more than just a temple, it is a symbol of endurance. The people who remember Asamai, who still whisper its name in reverence, they too endure. They are scholars, traders, warriors, men and women who remember a time before conquest dictated faith. They move through the land like the rivers, unseen yet shaping everything."

Kyra's gaze lifted to the sky, her thoughts racing. "Kandahar stands at a crossroads, does it not? A meeting of paths, of histories, of faiths."

"Yes," Kanak affirmed. "And in such places, knowledge is the true power. Those who control it shape the world. The temple was not only a spiritual refuge but also a place of learning. It held records, scriptures, maps of trade routes—things that could guide the wise and offer strength to those who understood them."

Aryanath turned to Kyra, his mind forming possibilities. "If the temple's knowledge still exists somewhere, it could help us understand not just the past, but the future of Kandahar."

Kanak's voice was steady. "But finding it will not be easy. The world is changing, and those who seek to control it do not wish for old knowledge to resurface."

Silence settled between them, a silence not of emptiness, but of contemplation. The Temple of Asamai was more than just a relic of the past; it was a thread that connected forgotten wisdom to the struggles of the present. And in that moment, Aryanath and Kyra knew—their journey had taken another turn, one that could define the fate of Kandahar itself.

Chapter 21 : Keepers of the Forgotten Path

The brazier's embers crackled softly, sending spirals of smoke into the night sky. Aryanath sat motionless, absorbing Kanak's words, while Kyra's gaze remained fixed on the flames, her mind tracing the path of forgotten histories. The Temple of Asamai, hidden in the folds of Kabul's rugged terrain, was more than a sanctuary—it was a repository of lost wisdom. And if knowledge was power, then the temple's survival, even in whispers, held a significance far greater than mere legend.

Kanak shifted slightly, the firelight casting deep shadows across his weathered face. "If you seek the temple, you must understand its keepers. They are not monks nor priests, not in the way temples are usually tended. The ones who guard its remnants are merchants, poets, and travellers. They do not wear robes, nor do they declare their faith openly. They walk among men unnoticed, yet their presence is everywhere."

Aryanath leaned forward, resting his elbows on his knees. "And where do we find them?"

Kanak smiled, his expression unreadable. "You don't. They find you."

A flicker of frustration crossed Aryanath's face, but Kyra spoke first.

"Are they waiting for something? Or someone?"

Kanak's gaze settled on her, his dark eyes reflecting a knowledge only long roads and forgotten stories could provide. "They wait for those who seek not wealth, nor dominion, but truth. And truth, Kyra, is a dangerous pursuit."

The words hung in the air like an unspoken warning.

Kyra straightened, her mind already moving beyond the present conversation. "What do you know of the temple's texts?" she asked. "You said they held maps, records, knowledge—what exactly remains?"

Kanak exhaled, the weight of time pressing into his voice. "It is said that within the temple, there were accounts of lands far beyond the Indus, of forgotten routes that once connected kingdoms now lost. Some say there were scrolls detailing the rise and fall of rulers, of battles fought in places few now remember. But most of all, there was knowledge of the stars, of time, and of the way men build their own destruction."

Aryanath's jaw tightened. "That knowledge could change everything."

"It could," Kanak agreed. "Or it could be buried forever, as so many truths before it."

A chill passed through the air, though the fire still burned.

Kyra turned to Aryanath, her voice steady.

"If the temple's guardians are still out there, if they still carry fragments of what was lost, we must reach them before others do."

Aryanath nodded. "We cannot let history repeat itself, where power silences wisdom."

Kanak watched them both carefully before he spoke again. "You wish to seek them out?"

"We do," Aryanath replied without hesitation.

Kanak studied them for a long moment before reaching into the folds of his shawl. From within, he pulled out a small, aged scroll, its edges worn, its parchment darkened with time. He held it up to the firelight, watching how the flame's glow danced upon its fragile surface.

"This," he said, "is the beginning of your path."

Kyra and Aryanath exchanged a glance

before Aryanath reached out, taking the scroll with careful hands.

Kanak's voice dropped to a near whisper. "But tread carefully. The ones who seek to erase the past are never far behind."

The fire crackled again, as if echoing the weight of his words.

Chapter 22: Echoes of the Ancient Land

The crisp air of the highlands carried with it the whispers of the past, as Aryanath and Kyra stood in the fading glow of the small fire. Kanak, his face illuminated by the flickering play of the fire they had just lit, took a slow breath before continuing his tale. The ancient land they stood upon was more than just dust and stone—it was a repository of forgotten truths, a witness to the rise and fall of empires, and the silent keeper of a culture that once thrived in the heart of the known world.

The Legacy of the Indo-Aryans

Kanak's voice carried a reverence that

was unmistakable. "Afghanistan," he began, "was once the epicenter of Vedic culture. The Indo-Aryans lived in these lands long before they migrated elsewhere, their legacy still buried beneath the soil and within the mountains that surround us. For them, this land was not ordinary—it was the realm of the Gandharvas, celestial beings of great knowledge and skill."

Aryanath's brow furrowed. "Gandharvas?"

Kanak nodded. "They were divine musicians, beings of magic and beauty. The Vedic scriptures describe them as neither mortal nor fully divine, yet they possessed powers beyond human comprehension.

Mischievous at times, but mostly benevolent, they were known for their wisdom and their role as intermediaries between gods and men. Afghanistan, in the minds of the Aryans, was a land where the sacred and the earthly intertwined. Even today, one can feel the weight of their presence in the echoes of forgotten hymns carried by the wind."

Kyra glanced toward the mountains, the jagged peaks standing like sentinels against the sky. "And yet, their presence is but a whisper now," she murmured.

Kanak's expression darkened. "Time has a way of burying history beneath the ruins of new empires. But in ancient times, these valleys must have been alive with the sound of caravans crisscrossing the land, bringing goods from the Indus Valley to the farthest reaches of the world."

The Crossroads of Civilisation

He gestured toward the distant horizon, where the land stretched into the unknown. "The Indus Valley people conducted overland trade through Afghanistan, connecting Mesopotamia with the riches of the East. This land was a crossroads—gold, silver, resins, spices, pistachios and incense all passed through here, carried by merchants who spoke in many tongues but understood the universal language of commerce."

Aryanath's mind raced as he envisioned the scene—traders leading their caravans through the rugged landscape, their camels laden with treasures, their eyes sharp as they navigated the perilous terrain. He could almost hear the sounds of their voices, the creak of wooden wheels, the rhythmic padding of hooves on packed earth.

"But trade was only one part of the story," Kanak continued. "This was also a land of ideas. The teachings of the Vedas, the wisdom of ancient scholars, and the knowledge of distant lands all converged here. Philosophers, astronomers, and seekers of truth walked these paths long before the great kingdoms of today ever laid claim to these lands."

Kyra's gaze sharpened. "And yet, it has been turned into a battlefield for centuries."

Kanak sighed. "Yes. The very wealth and significance of this land made it a prize for conquerors. But beneath the ruins, beneath the bloodstained fields, the essence of its ancient spirit remains. Those who listen closely can still hear it."

Unraveling the Forgotten Threads

Aryanath took a deep breath, feeling the weight of history pressing upon him. "If this land holds such deep wisdom, why has it been forgotten?"

Kanak looked toward the darkening sky. "Perhaps because true wisdom is often buried beneath the ambitions of men. But that does not mean it is lost forever. It is up to those who seek it to uncover it again."

Silence settled between them, heavy with unspoken thoughts. The journey ahead was not just one of survival—it was a quest to reclaim something ancient, something sacred. Aryanath and Kyra exchanged a glance, understanding passing between them.

The past was not merely a collection of old stories. It was alive, waiting to be remembered.

And they would be its keepers.

Chapter 23: The Gathering Storm

Dawn broke over the rugged landscape of Kandahar, casting long golden streaks across the sky. The cold night had surrendered to a crisp morning, and the air carried the scent of damp earth, mingled with the lingering aroma of burnt wood from the dying embers of their campfire. Aryanath sat in silence, his gaze fixed on the horizon where the first slivers of sunlight illuminated the temple ruins in the distance. Kyra stood nearby, wrapping her shawl tightly around her shoulders, her face pensive as the memories of the previous night weighed heavily upon her.

Kanak, who had spent much of the night speaking about the history of Asamai, now crouched near the fire, carefully stoking the embers. His voice had carried the weight of generations, and even now, as the morning light spread, his expression remained solemn. The knowledge he had shared was not just words—it was the truth of a world long buried under the shifting sands of time.

"We must move," Aryanath finally spoke, breaking the silence that had settled over them. "We have lingered long enough."

Kyra turned to him, her eyes searching his face. "And yet, it feels as if we have only just begun to understand what truly lies ahead."

Kanak nodded in agreement. "The past is a river, ever flowing, shaping the land and carving new paths. But today, the current runs swift, and we must choose whether to move with it or be drowned beneath its force."

They gathered their belongings swiftly, their movements careful yet efficient. The weight of responsibility hung heavy upon their shoulders, but there was no room for hesitation.

As they descended from the high ground, the city of Kandahar spread before them like a living tapestry of stone and dust. The streets, already coming alive with traders and travellers, carried whispers of change. Soldiers from various factions moved cautiously, their armour glinting in the morning sun. Tensions had been brewing, and the shifting power dynamics had set an uneasy undercurrent in motion.

"The rulers grow restless," Kanak observed as they passed a group of armed men standing near a well, their hushed voices betraying concern. "They know something is coming, even if they do not yet understand its form."

Kyra's brow furrowed. "The fall of empires is rarely sudden—it begins in the hearts of the people before it ever reaches the walls of a city."

Aryanath glanced at her. "Then we must be ahead of the tide. What we have learned must not be lost to history. If the temple's secrets hold any answers, we must ensure they are not buried in the chaos that follows war."

Their steps carried them toward the market district, where the scent of spices and fresh bread momentarily broke the tension in the air. But the respite was brief. A sudden commotion erupted near the city gates, drawing their attention.

A group of travellers had arrived, their robes tattered from the road, their faces weary but resolute. Among them was a man draped in the insignia of a distant land—a scholar, by the looks of him, carrying a scroll that bore the mark of an unfamiliar seal.

Aryanath and Kyra exchanged a glance. The past had spoken through Kanak, but now the future called to them in ways they could not yet comprehend.

"We must listen," Kyra murmured.

"And we must act," Aryanath replied.

With that, they stepped forward into the gathering storm.

Chapter 24: Echoes of the Unwritten

The morning sun had fully risen, casting its warm glow over the bustling streets of Kandahar. The city was alive, but there was something uneasy in the air, a tension that clung to the conversations in the marketplace and the guarded expressions of the travellers passing through.

Aryanath, Kyra, and Kanak moved cautiously, their eyes fixed on the commotion near the city gates. The newly arrived travellers, dressed in worn but once-fine robes, stood in a loose circle, their leader clutching a scroll adorned with an unfamiliar seal. His presence alone demanded attention, but it was the way he held himself—poised, deliberate, aware of every movement around him—that made Aryanath wary.

"Who are they?" Kyra whispered, keeping her voice low.

"Scholars," Kanak replied, his gaze sharp. "Or messengers. Either way, they bring knowledge—or warnings."

As they drew closer, the murmurs of the crowd grew louder. The leader of the traveler, a man of middle years with streaks of grey in his dark beard, unrolled the scroll and began to speak.

"The world is changing." His voice was deep, unwavering. "The Caliphate weakens, and the lands of the east and west stir with new ambition. The cities that once flourished under peace now tremble under the weight of war. Trade routes will be redrawn, and knowledge will either be preserved—or lost."

A hush fell over the gathering. The man's words were not simply declarations; they were warnings.

Kyra stepped forward, her royal bearing unmistakable. "Who sent you?" she asked.

The scholar turned his gaze to her, eyes dark as ink on parchment. "We come from the House of Wisdom in Baghdad," he said. "But we do not speak for the Caliph. We are seekers of truth, and we have seen the tides of history shift before."

Aryanath folded his arms. "And what truth do you bring to Kandahar?"

The scholar took a breath, as if weighing his words. "That those who hold knowledge must guard it well. That temples, libraries, and scholars will be the first to fall when war comes—not to steel, but to silence."

A chill passed through Kyra. She had seen the destruction of knowledge before— seen how fire and greed could erase centuries of wisdom in mere days.

Kanak stepped forward. "The Temple of Asamai still holds secrets, secrets even the Caliphate does not fully understand. If war reaches Kandahar, what do you propose?"

The scholar's gaze settled on him.

"Preservation. You must gather what you can, ensure it is safeguarded, and, if necessary, hidden away from those who would see it lost."

Aryanath exhaled slowly. The weight of history pressed against him. He had always known their mission was greater than themselves, but now the urgency was undeniable.

"Then we must act swiftly," Kyra said.

The scholar nodded. "And wisely."

The group dispersed, but the warning lingered in the air like a ghost. As Aryanath, Kyra, and Kanak moved through the streets once more, the reality of their task settled heavily upon them. The past was whispering, the future was uncertain, and the present demanded action.

Would they be fast enough to save what must not be lost?

They had no choice but to try.

Chapter 25: Guardians of the Unseen

The weight of responsibility pressed upon Aryanath and Kyra as they walked through the winding alleys of Kandahar, their minds reeling from the scholar's warning. The morning air, once crisp and invigorating, now felt heavy, as if the city itself understood the peril that lay ahead.

Kanak walked beside them, his young face thoughtful. "If they have come from the House of Wisdom," he said, "then the situation must be dire.

Baghdad is the heart of knowledge, yet even they fear its destruction."

Kyra's jaw tightened. "History repeats itself. Knowledge has always been the first casualty of war. It is not enough for conquerors to claim power—they must erase the wisdom of those before them."

Aryanath remained silent, his thoughts drifting to the Temple of Asamai, to the vast knowledge hidden within its walls. The temple was more than a place of worship; it was a vault of history, philosophy, and ancient wisdom passed down for generations. If Kandahar fell, it would be lost.

They reached a quieter part of the city, where the air carried the scent of old parchment and ink. Aryanath led them into a modest but well-guarded building—the Chamber of Commerce's inner sanctum. Within its walls, merchants, scribes, and traders met to discuss the affairs of the city, their decisions shaping the economy of Kandahar.

Inside, a small group of scholars and elders awaited them. Among them was an aged man with piercing eyes and a steady voice—Elder Pravar, one of the keepers of Kandahar's history.

"We received word of the messengers,"

Elder Pravar said. "Their warning cannot be ignored. If the winds of war reach us, our knowledge must be protected."

Kanak stepped forward. "The temple holds more than just spiritual records. There are scrolls, maps, and accounts of ancient civilisations. If they are lost, we lose more than history—we lose guidance for the future."

Aryanath met Elder Pravar's gaze. "Then we must act now. We need to gather what we can and find a way to secure it."

Pravar nodded. "There is a vault beneath the temple, one that has not been opened in decades. It was built in an age when kings feared invaders would burn the city to the ground. If the temple is at risk, the vault must be used."

Kyra frowned. "If it has been sealed for so long, how can we be sure it is still intact?"

A new voice answered from the shadows. "We cannot. But we have no other choice."

From the corner of the room, a man emerged—Darius. He had been listening silently, his expression unreadable. "If the scholars from Baghdad believe their libraries are in danger, then war is closer than we think." His gaze moved to Aryanath. "The real question is: are you ready to do what is necessary to save it?"

Aryanath exhaled slowly. Ready or not, they had no choice.

"Gather those you trust," he said. "Tonight, we open the vault."

A hush fell over the room. The course of history was shifting, and they were at its heart.

As the sun climbed higher over Kandahar, Aryanath knew that the coming night would mark the beginning of a battle—not with swords and shields, but with time and fate itself.

Chapter 26: The Vault Beneath the Temple

The journey from Kandahar to Kabul stretched over two long days, their path winding through treacherous landscapes, steep mountain passes, and vast, desolate plains. The sky above them remained an endless canopy of stars at night, while the sun burned fiercely during the day, casting long, wavering shadows across the dunes.

With each passing hour, the weight of their mission pressed heavier upon their shoulders. But what lay ahead in the depths of the Temple of Asamai—buried beneath decades of dust and forgotten time—could rewrite everything.

Darius remained silent throughout the journey, his face concealed beneath a dark hood and mask. He had kept to the shadows, offering neither his name nor his past, only his skill and guidance. Yet, his presence was undeniable, an unspoken force that watched over them with calculated precision.

But the weight on his heart was far greater than any of them knew.

His eyes often lingered on Kyra when she wasn't looking. The way she studied every detail of the land around them, her mind constantly working through the unknown, her presence both commanding and enigmatic.

There was something about her—something that made him question his own resolve.

But he knew his place.

And this was not his time.

Arrival at the Temple of Asamai

The city of Kabul rose before them like a silent sentinel, nestled between the rugged hills, its ancient walls bearing the weight of untold stories. Unlike the bustling trade routes of Kandahar, Kabul was a city of whispered secrets, where knowledge had survived in the hidden corners of its temples and the ink-stained hands of its scholars.

The Temple of Asamai loomed above them, its stone walls etched with the faded inscriptions of celestial beings—guardians of a world long lost to time. The entrance stood tall and unyielding, its doors weathered by centuries, yet still possessing an air of defiance.

As they climbed the winding path leading to the temple, the early morning sun bathed the landscape in a golden hue, the first rays stretching like fingers across the earth. A sense of urgency filled the air, for they knew that what lay beyond those walls had remained untouched for decades, perhaps even centuries.

The weight of history itself seemed to press upon them as they crossed the threshold.

Unveiling the Vault

The inner sanctum of the temple was vast, its grand columns rising toward the heavens, their intricate carvings whispering of an era when gods and men walked together. The air was thick with the scent of aged parchment and burning incense, remnants of a time when knowledge had been sacred.

At the centre of the chamber, the floor bore a magnificent mosaic, its patterns intricate yet fragmented. Raunaka knelt before it, his aged fingers tracing the worn edges.

"This," he whispered, "is the key."

Darius stepped forward without a word, retrieving an ancient bronze emblem from within his cloak. He examined the small indentation at the heart of the mosaic before pressing the emblem into its place.

For a moment, nothing happened.

Then, the ground beneath them trembled.

A low, mechanical groan echoed through the chamber as dust rained down from the ceiling. The mosaic split apart, revealing a hidden stone slab embedded into the earth. Slowly, it began to shift, rotating with a deep, guttural sound.

The vault was opening.

An icy gust of air rushed from the darkness below, carrying with it the scent of something untouched by time—of ink-stained pages, of whispered secrets, of history itself awakening from its slumber.

As they descended the spiral staircase into the vault's depths, the silence grew heavier, pressing against them like the weight of forgotten civilisations.

And then they saw it.

The chamber stretched far beyond what their torches could illuminate. Scrolls, tablets, and ancient tomes lined the walls, their bindings still strong, their words still waiting to be read. Bronze and gold lamps stood in the corners, untouched by time. The sheer magnitude of knowledge stored here was staggering.

Kyra's breath hitched as she ran her fingers across the fragile pages of a manuscript. "These... these texts predate the scholars of Baghdad."

Raunaka's hands trembled as he knelt beside her. "This is the wisdom of a world before history was written. The knowledge of civilisations that were erased by time. The voices of those who fought to preserve it."

Kanak's voice was hushed, reverent. "This must be protected."

The Disguise of Merchants

Time was against them. They knew they could not linger. Carefully, they gathered what they could—manuscripts that held the secrets of lost worlds, scrolls that spoke of those who had fought to preserve the truth. Each piece was a fragment of a forgotten puzzle, one that, if placed together, could reshape their understanding of the past.

They wrapped the scrolls in cloth, tying them into bundles that would not draw suspicion. With swift precision, they disguised themselves in the garments of traveling merchants, the scent of nutmeg, cumin, and cloves masking the truth of their mission.

As they emerged from the temple, the streets of Kabul bustled with traders and buyers. They blended seamlessly into the crowd, their voices rising with the others as they called out to passersby.

"Spices from Kandahar! Fresh nutmeg, cumin, and cloves!"

Their deception was flawless. They sold twenty kilograms of spices, their wares exchanged for coin, their movements nothing more than those of merchants seeking trade.

But as they unloaded their horses, preparing to leave the city, a figure approached them.

A man, his robe simple yet his posture deliberate, his eyes sharp with understanding.

He did not hesitate as he stepped closer.

"Are you the saviours of knowledge?" he asked, his voice a mere whisper. "Were you sent by the House of Wisdom?"

Kyra met his gaze, unflinching. She understood immediately.

He was one of them.

Her voice was steady. "Guard the Temple of Asamai at any cost. Do it with your community. Protect it, for it is the only place where history will remain alive."

The man bowed his head, his expression one of silent resolve. "It will be done."

No further words were spoken. None were needed.

The Departure

As Kyra, Aryanath, Darius, Raunaka, and Kanak rode from Kabul, the bundles of wisdom secured to their saddlebags, the weight of their journey settled deep within them.

Darius remained at the rear, his eyes lingering on Kyra one last time. He knew his role was not yet complete.

But it was not his time to stay.

Without a word, as they neared the edge of the city, he pulled his horse to a halt. The others barely noticed, their focus on the path ahead.

And just like that, he disappeared into the shadows.

Kyra turned once, her brow furrowing as if sensing something amiss. But the moment passed, and she pressed forward.

The road to Kandahar awaited.

And with them, they carried the gems of wisdom—the voices of the past that would guide the future.

Chapter 27: The Weight of Knowledge

The road to Kandahar stretched before them, winding through the vast expanse of rugged terrain and shifting sands. The horses moved at a steady pace, their hooves kicking up dust as the sun began its descent, painting the sky in streaks of crimson and gold.

The air was thick with the scent of earth and spice, remnants of their disguise lingering on their cloaks. But beneath the veil of merchant garb, they carried something far more valuable than any commodity—knowledge, salvaged from the depths of time.

Kyra rode at the front, her mind racing with the implications of what they had uncovered in the Temple of Asamai. The vault had held not just books and scrolls but entire worlds of thought—wisdom predating even the great libraries of Baghdad. It was a history that had been deliberately buried, hidden away from the reach of empires that sought to erase the past to control the future.

Aryanath rode beside her, his expression unreadable. He had seen how empires rose and fell, how rulers rewrote history to serve their own legacies. But what they had now... it was proof that truth could survive, if only in the hands of those willing to protect it.

Kanak and Raunaka trailed slightly behind, their voices murmuring in quiet discussion, debating the significance of certain manuscripts. Some texts spoke of lands beyond the known world, others of philosophies lost to time, and some detailed strategies that had once been wielded by rulers who refused to bow to tyranny.

And then there was Darius.

Or rather, the absence of him.

Kyra had felt it the moment he had disappeared. No words, no farewell—just silence, swallowed by the shadows of Kabul.

A part of her had known he would not stay.

But that did not mean she understood why.

She turned slightly, glancing toward Aryanath, whose gaze was locked on the horizon. He, too, had sensed it.

"You expected him to leave," she finally said.

Aryanath did not answer immediately. Instead, he let out a slow breath, the wind catching the loose strands of his hair.

The absence of Darius gnawed at her, an unfinished thought that would not leave her mind. She had never known him well—his presence had been like a passing storm, sudden yet lingering. But there was something about the way he had helped them, the way he had disappeared without a word, that unsettled her.

"Why did he leave?" she asked, her voice barely above a whisper. "After everything?"

Aryanath keeping a tight rein on, was choosing his words carefully. Then, without looking at her, he said, "Before we left Kandahar, Pravar told me about him. He said, 'This man is loyal beyond reason. He asks for nothing, yet he will give everything. Keep him. He has no chains, no ties, no master. He chooses when to appear and when to disappear. He will help you when you least expect it.'"

Kyra frowned. "Then why hide his face? Why not tell us his name?"

Aryanath looked down. "That, Pravar did not say. Only that he has both knowledge and tactics—qualities that make him dangerous to those who seek to control men like him. He is not someone who serves out of duty. He serves because he chooses to. And that makes him more powerful than any other man."

Kyra's fingers tightened around the fabric of her cloak. There was something unsettling about that kind of loyalty—the kind that came without demand, without expectation. It was rare. And it was dangerous.

"Do you trust him?" she asked finally.

Aryanath met her gaze, his voice steady. "I trust that he will return when the time is right."

A silence settled between them.

Aryanath's grip tightened on the reins.

There was something deeper in his voice—something unspoken. But before Kyra could press further, Kanak's voice broke through the tension.

"These texts," Kanak said, shifting his saddlebag, "they speak of knowledge as both salvation and destruction."

Kyra and Aryanath turned toward him.

Kanak's brow was furrowed as he

continued, "The vault held not just wisdom, but warnings. Every empire that thrived on knowledge also suffered because of it. The moment rulers saw it as a weapon rather than a guide, they burned libraries, slaughtered scholars, and erased entire civilisations. They rewrote history to fit their own narrative, leaving only fragments behind."

Raunaka, ever the quiet observer, nodded in agreement. "We have seen this before. From Alexandria to Persia, from Nalanda to Baghdad—whenever knowledge grew too powerful, it was either hidden or destroyed. What we hold now... it is dangerous."

Kyra felt the weight of his words settle deep in her chest. "And yet," she said, her voice steady, "if we do not preserve it, then the truth dies with us."

Aryanath nodded. "That is why we must decide carefully. Where to keep it. Who to trust."

Kanak sighed. "And who to hide it from."

The Road Through the Highlands

The path ahead grew steeper, leading them into the highlands where the air was crisp, and the winds carried the scent of pine and damp earth. The terrain shifted from open desert to rugged hills, a stark reminder of the changing lands they traversed.

As night began to fall, they found shelter in the hollow of a cliffside, where the rocks provided cover from the cold winds. A fire crackled between them, casting long shadows across the stone walls.

It was here, beneath the vast sky littered with stars, that the weight of their journey truly settled upon them.

Raunaka unwrapped one of the scrolls they had retrieved, his fingers tracing the inked lines with reverence. "This speaks of a time before kings and conquerors, before the written word dictated law. A time when wisdom was shared, not hoarded."

Kanak shook his head. "And yet, here we are, centuries later, fighting the same battle. Knowledge remains chained—either by those who seek to suppress it or those who seek to control it."

Kyra looked around the fire, her gaze meeting each of theirs in turn. "Then we must become something different. Not rulers, not warriors... but guardians."

Aryanath exhaled, his expression unreadable. "And where do guardians keep their treasures, Kyra?"

She paused, the answer already forming in her mind.

"Kandahar."

It was a bold declaration, one that carried both promise and peril. But Kandahar was not just a city; it was a crossroads, a place where cultures, ideas, and traditions converged.

If knowledge was to be protected, it needed to be somewhere untouchable.

Aryanath considered her words carefully. "Then we must prepare. There will be those who seek to claim it for themselves. Those who will kill to possess it."

Raunaka closed the scroll, his eyes heavy with understanding. "We will need allies. And we will need secrecy."

Kyra's jaw tightened. "Then secrecy is what we shall have."

Kanak leaned forward, his voice quieter now. "But if we are to do this, if we are to become the keepers of knowledge... then we must understand that we are painting a target on our backs. And on Kandahar itself."

A silence fell over the group.

The fire crackled between them, the only sound in the stillness of the night.

And then, finally, Aryanath spoke.

"If we do this," he said, his voice like tempered steel, "then there is no turning back."

Kyra met his gaze.

"There never was."

Unbeknownst to them, beyond the edge of the fire's glow, a lone figure stood in the darkness, watching. His mask concealed all but his eyes, sharp and knowing.

Darius had not truly left them.

Not yet.

From the shadows, he listened. He understood.

And as the wind carried their voices across the highlands, he made a silent vow.

When the time was right, he would return.

Not as a stranger.

But as something far more.

A reckoning.

Chapter 28: Shadows of the Unwritten Future

The journey back to Kandahar was marked by an eerie stillness, as if the desert itself had absorbed the weight of what they had uncovered. The wind howled through the dunes, whispering secrets that had remained buried for centuries. The knowledge they carried was not just fragile—it was dangerous. If it fell into the wrong hands, it could rewrite the fate of kingdoms.

Kyra rode in silence, her mind circling the past few days like a predator tracking prey. Every answer they had found had only birthed more questions. What lay ahead for them now? The history they had unraveled, the vault they had opened—it was more than just an act of discovery. It was an act of defiance against forces that had tried to erase it from existence.

Raunaka rode beside her, his usual cheer subdued. Even Kanak, who had brought them the first whispers of this forgotten past, now seemed lost in thought. But it was Aryanath whose silence weighed the heaviest.

Kyra turned to him, studying the hard set of his jaw, the way his grip on the reins never loosened, as if he feared that if he let go for even a moment, everything would spiral out of control.

"You haven't said a word since we left," she said finally.

Aryanath kept his eyes forward. "What is there to say?"

Kyra narrowed her gaze. "Everything. You always have something to say."

A muscle in his jaw twitched. For a moment, it seemed as if he would dismiss her with his usual restraint, but then he exhaled sharply. "What we did back there, Kyra... It was not just about uncovering the past. It was about rewriting what was lost." His voice was low, edged with something unreadable. "And history has shown that those who try to rewrite the past often find themselves consumed by it."

Kyra frowned, feeling the weight of his words settle over her. "Do you regret it?"

Aryanath turned to her then, his dark eyes meeting hers in the dimming light. "Never." His voice was steady, unwavering. "But it changes everything. We are no longer just seekers of knowledge. We are its guardians now. And that means the battle ahead will not just be fought with swords."

Kyra felt the truth of his words deep in her bones. Knowledge was power. And power invited enemies.

By the time they reached Kandahar, the scent of spice and burning wood greeted them, a contrast to the cold, ancient air of Asamai. The city was alive, unaware of the weight these travellers carried upon their shoulders.

But as they passed through the gates,

Aryanath felt it—an unease, a shift in the air. Something had changed.

A rider approached them in haste, his horse kicking up dust as he pulled to a sharp halt before them. His face was shadowed by exhaustion, his clothes stained with the wear of a hard ride.

"My lord," the rider addressed Aryanath directly, breathless. "There has been an attack. The western outposts—burned to the ground."

Kyra's fingers clenched around the reins, her pulse quickening.

Aryanath remained still, his face unreadable. "By whom?"

The rider swallowed hard. "We don't know. But they left a message—written in the sand before the flames consumed it."

Aryanath's voice was low, controlled. "And what did it say?"

The rider met his gaze. "That the war for knowledge has already begun."

A silence fell over the group. The shadows of an unwritten future loomed before them, and somewhere, in the distance, beyond the walls of Kandahar, an enemy had already made their move.

Chapter 29: The Burden of Time

The nights in Kandahar had grown tense, the air thick with the weight of looming war. Within the temple walls, Kyra and Aryanath moved swiftly, their hands careful as they gathered relics and scrolls, preparing them for the hidden passage that led to safety. The distant sounds of the Seleucid forces settling into their camps haunted the night, a reminder that time was running out.

"They're closer," Aryanath said quietly, his voice steady despite the fear that tightened his features.

"The temple is prepared, and Kyra has hidden some of the relics, but we're running out of time."

Rajvanta nodded, his jaw clenched. "This city has stood for centuries, Aryanath. It will not fall while I still have breath in my body."

As they spoke, Bhadrasen arrived, leaning heavily on his walking staff, his face a mask of grim acceptance. Though age had wearied him, he still carried the dignity of a scholar, a keeper of truth.

"I have lived long enough to see empires rise and fall," Bhadrasen said, his voice deep and resonant. "Yet this city, this land, has endured. It is made of something far stronger than stone or steel. But, Rajvanta," he continued, turning to the warrior, "we must be wise as well as brave. If we are to survive, we must protect what we can."

A silence settled between them, thick with unsaid words. Outside, the city groaned under the weight of inevitability. Somewhere in the distance, a temple bell tolled—a slow, measured sound, neither warning nor mourning, merely an acknowledgment of time slipping past them, uncaring.

Rajvanta exhaled sharply. "We fight with what we have," he said. "But war is more than swords. If the city is to endure, we must think beyond this night."

Kyra adjusted the leather strap of the satchel slung across her shoulder. It was filled with scrolls, parchments inscribed with the knowledge of those who had come before them— records of trade, of treaties, of ancient wisdom that could not be rewritten once lost. She had chosen carefully, leaving behind what could be replaced, taking only what time could not restore.

"The temple's history cannot fall into their hands," she said. "They seek to conquer land, but knowledge is the true prize. If we are to fight, we strike where they least expect."

Aryanath's fingers curled into fists at his sides. The great stone doors of the temple stood sealed for now, but the enemy would come, and they would come soon. His gaze flickered to Bhadrasen. There was something the old scholar wasn't saying.

"You know another way," Aryanath said. It was not a question.

Bhadrasen did not flinch. "There is a passage," he admitted. "Older than the temple itself. It runs beneath the city, carved into stone before even the first kings. Few know of it."

Rajvanta's head snapped toward him. "And you have kept this hidden?"

"Because it was never meant for war," Bhadrasen replied. "It was meant for preservation. There are moments in history when knowledge, not steel, must survive. This is one of them."

Kyra's breath hitched. "You want us to leave?"

The old scholar's gaze did not waver. "I want you to endure."

The words settled deep, heavier than the threat outside. The idea of leaving—of stepping away while others stood their ground—felt like betrayal. And yet, what was the purpose of war if nothing remained after?

The sound came then—a sharp, splintering crack against the heavy doors. The first strike. A pause. Then another. Wood groaned, dust trembled from the walls. The Seleucids had come.

Rajvanta's hand went to his sword. "There is no time."

Aryanath turned to Bhadrasen. "Where is the passage?"

The old man gestured toward the far wall. "There."

Kyra moved first, her steps quick, determined. No hesitation. Aryanath followed, but not before casting one last look at Rajvanta.

"Hold them," he said. "Buy us the time we need."

Rajvanta nodded once. "Go."

The doors shuddered again. The sound of steel being unsheathed filled the chamber.

Then, the wall gave way, revealingdarkness beyond. The scent of old earth, undisturbed for centuries, filled the air.

They stepped through, and the stone sealed behind them.

Chapter 30: Echoes of the Past

The stone door sealed shut behind them with a final, echoing thud, drowning out the chaos of the world above. Kyra stood in the dark, her breath shallow, listening. No sound from the other side—no desperate pounding, no shouts of retreat. Only silence.

Aryanath lit a small oil lamp, the flickering flame casting long, uneasy shadows across the walls of the ancient tunnel. The air was damp, thick with the scent of earth that had been undisturbed for centuries. The passage stretched ahead, carved stone leading downward, into the unknown.

Kanak and Raunaka had made their choice. They had remained at the gates of the Temple, standing resolute against the inevitable tide. Their decision had been wordless, understood in a single glance exchanged before the entrance had been sealed. There had been no farewell—only the quiet certainty of duty.

Aryanath's grip tightened around the satchel slung across his back, its weight pressing against him with every step. Within it lay the scrolls from the Temple of Asamai—fragments of wisdom that had survived countless lifetimes, now entrusted to their hands.

"How long do you think they can hold them off?" Kyra's voice was quiet, but there was no hiding the weight behind it.

Aryanath did not look at her. "Long enough," he said, though even he was unsure if it was a promise or a prayer.

They pressed forward, each step pulling them further from the city above—the only home they had ever known.

A sudden tremor rumbled through the stone, a deep, angry groan from the world above. Dust rained down from the ceiling. The battle had begun in earnest.

Aryanath exchanged a glance with Kyra. "Faster."

They pressed on, their feet echoing against the stone as they moved through the winding tunnel. The further they went, the colder the air became, until the warmth of the temple above felt like nothing more than a distant memory.

At last, the passage opened into a vast underground chamber. The lamplight flickered across towering stone shelves, each filled with scrolls and relics wrapped in layers of cloth. A hidden archive—untouched, unseen for generations.

Kyra stepped forward, awestruck. "This... this is more than just a refuge."

Aryanath moved to the centre of the chamber, his breath steadying. "Then we protect it."

But before another word could be spoken, another tremor shook the chamber. This time, it was stronger. The earth above them groaned under the weight of war.

Kyra's stomach twisted. "We can still—"

"No," Aryanath interrupted, his voice calm but firm. "What is above will fall. But what is here must remain."

Another tremor, this time violent enough to send scrolls tumbling from their shelves. The city was breaking. Time was running out.

Kyra reached into her satchel, pulling out the scrolls from the Temple of Asamai. She placed them carefully on one of the shelves, her fingers lingering over the parchment.

"We are not the first to do this," she said softly. "And we won't be the last."

Aryanath looked at her, seeing not just the scholar she had become, but the future she now carried. The weight of the past, the burden of knowledge—it would not end with them.

"We seal the chamber," he said. "If the city is lost, this will remain."

They moved quickly, working to ensure that the archive would survive even if the city did not.

Stones were shifted, barriers placed, the passage concealed once more beneath centuries of secrecy.

By the time they finished, the tremors had slowed. The sounds of war above had dulled into eerie silence.

Aryanath turned to Kyra, his expression unreadable. "Are you ready?"

She met his gaze, understanding passing between them like an unspoken oath. "We walk forward," she said. "Because that is what history demands."

And so they did.

Through the darkness of the tunnel, they

walked toward the unknown, carrying with them the past of a city that would never be forgotten.

Far above, Kandahar burned.

And deep below, its truth endured.

As the dust of centuries settled, as empires rose and fell, the hidden chamber remained.

Until one day, when the world above would seek the past once more, and the echoes of the Mortals of Kandahar would be heard again...